THE WITCHES
OF THE
CROSSWORLDS

BOOK III
FUTURE HISTORY

The Witches of the Crossworlds
Book III
Future History
Copyright © 2023 by Graham Anthony Davidson

ISBN: paperback 978-0-6459286-2-4
Second edition
First published 2022
Special thanks to all those who have contributed with their feedback
and support throughout the writing of these books.,

Published by Rack and Rune Publishing
rackandrune.com
email: info@rackandrune.com

... the correct way to view time is like this, with all points co-existing together. There is little relevance as to what is future or past unless you are sitting somewhere within that line. From outside the line, it's all one and the same moment.

Krinkle-myst

PROLOGUE

C aptain Taylor closed his eyes and took a deep breath before he entered Governor Pritchard's office. The Nasqa, or mind thief, possessing the captain's body was unaccustomed to feeling such emotions. He'd never experienced anything like anxiety until his humiliation before a justice of the peace at Colin McIntyre's trial twelve months earlier.

Nothing could have prepared him for this, though. The gravedigger, Sean O'Malley, sat in a chair across from the Governor. He was well groomed, wearing new clothing, smoking a cigar, and drinking a brandy. He stood up and extended his hand to the Captain. "What a wonderful day it is, made all the better for us being re-united."

Captain Taylor feigned a smile as he accepted O'Malley's limp and clammy hand for the briefest of moments before turning his attention back to his host. "Governor, it's a great honour to be summoned here today."

Governor Pritchard took a generous drag on his cigar, then gestured toward an empty chair. "Angus, my dear friend, take a seat. And for God's sake man, can we dispense with the formalities? Please, call me Charles." He grabbed the brandy decanter and poured a generous glass, which he handed to the Captain. Then he opened the cigar box on his desk. "Cigar?"

"No, thank you."

The Governor brought his hands together and cracked his knuckles before placing his feet up on his desk. "I can't begin to tell you how pleased I am that you could both make it today." He grinned as he watched the two men before him cast a nervous glance toward each other. He leaned back, looked toward the door to an adjoining office, and called out, "Gladys, you can come in now."

Mrs Gladys Bradshaw shuffled into the room with her eyes cast down. Her clothing was soiled, the flesh on her face and arms covered in grime.

The governor stood up and walked around the desk. "Gentlemen, I'd like you to meet Gladys Bradshaw." He put his arm around Gladys's shoulder and hugged her tight. "Widow, and former host to one of our kind." He brushed a lock of hair from in front of her eye. "One who fell victim to the pixies while performing her duty on our behalf at the McIntyre property." He looked down at the two men seated before him. "That was just on two years ago." He rested his forehead against the side of the widow's head. "The poor woman, losing all the power that went with her symbiotic relationship to our kin. The whole ordeal sent her quite mad." He took hold of her chin and turned her face to his. "You'd love to feel that power and security again, wouldn't you Gladys?"

The woman nodded then cast her eyes downward once more.

Governor Pritchard clapped his hands together as he moved away from her. "And this, gentlemen, is where you two can be of great help." He pointed to O'Malley. "You, Sean, have made no secret of your desire, your desperation even, for a host of higher station."

O'Malley looked to his feet as he shook his head, then, with a grim expression and a tear welling in his eye, he looked at the Governor. "I'm sorry, Your Governance, sir..." He looked away and his lower jaw trembled with no words coming out. *I have to say it*, he thought. *It won't change anything, but I have to say it.* He closed his eyes and shook his head. "It's just that I'm struggling... I'm struggling to see how there is much of a betterment in going from a gravedigger"—his eyes betrayed his dread when he opened them and stared at Gladys—"to a mentally deranged widow."

The governor smiled and stepped forward to be between the two men in their chairs. He squatted and put his arms around their shoulders. "Ah, but this is where it gets really good for you, Sean. You see, Mrs Bradshaw's station will soon be much higher." He turned to the Captain to make sure he was paying attention, then back to O'Malley, "That is, once she's married to the Captain, to the Captain of Springwood Barracks." His eyes sparkled with joy as he grinned at O'Malley. "By this time tomorrow, you'll be known as Mrs Gladys Taylor." He gave O'Malley a gentle punch in the shoulder. "You lucky old dog, you."

O'Malley cast his eyes toward Gladys, then glared at the Captain before turning his gaze back to the Governor. "And what's the benefit for yourself in this?"

The Governor straightened up. "You men are both familiar with the McIntyre property?"

The two men nodded in grim silence.

The Governor looked at the Captain. "Wouldn't you just love to have the sweet taste of revenge against the father of that family? What was his name?" He looked up snapping his fingers. "Ah, that's it." He turned back to the Captain. "Colin, Colin McIntyre. I know I certainly want revenge. There were a great many Nasqa who gave up on this world thanks to that family... not to mention our kin who ended up lost in the void."

Captain Taylor grimaced, his fingers massaging his forehead as the proposition the Governor had put forward swirled around his head. "Begging your pardon, Governor—"

"It's Charles. Just call me Charles."

"Begging your pardon, Charles, but there wouldn't be any need for me to get my revenge if it weren't for this lying scumbag here that you want to marry me off to."

The Governor leaned back and spread out his hands. "But don't you see? That's why this plan is such a good one. It was no secret that you two had a bit of trouble getting on with each other during all that kerfuffle last year. And the way I see it, you both bear some of the responsibility. I mean, really Angus, you did get a little bit nasty toward Sean. And Sean, you could've shown Angus here a tad more respect. After all, he is a captain and all. You can both see this as your chance to make amends. A fresh start."

A grin spread across the Governor's face as he tried to pick which of the two appeared more horrified. It was days like this when he derived the most pleasure from inhabiting this particular host.

O'Malley asked, "I'm just wondering what might be the rest of your plan. Do you have something specific in mind that you wish us to do to them?"

The governor snapped his fingers and pointed at O'Malley. "Very good question, Sean." He glanced across to the Captain. "See, Angus, Sean's already taking up the initiative. You'll make a wonderful team."

Captain Taylor closed his eyes in the hope it might somehow take him away from the situation. The Governor said, "I do indeed have a plan."

He opened a draw in his desk, pulled out a glass jar, and placed it in the middle of his desk. On first glance, it appeared empty. But when the Captain and O'Malley leaned forward for a closer look, they noticed some movement. There was a type of worm at the bottom of the jar that had the shape of a large leech, but refracted the light so it appeared transparent as though it were made of glass. The Captain looked up at the Governor. "Is that what I think it is?"

The Governor sat in his chair, leaned back, and put his feet up on the desk while having a quiet chuckle to himself.

O'Malley focused his attention on the jar as he whispered, "Tickle me pink if that isn't a stringworm."

CHAPTER 1

A magpie warbled. Miss Clara Jenkins smiled and looked around the treetops for where the bird might be as she and Patsy continued down the sandstone path. They descended further, then wound past an old fig tree that revealed the first glimpse of their destination. A pool expanded out from a bend in the otherwise narrow and fast flowing stream weaving through the southern end of the McIntyre property. A gentle mist rose from the icy water as its surface was caressed by the morning sunshine streaming through the tallest of the eucalyptus trees. It was a warm day, unusual for the middle of winter, made all the more magical by the sweet melody of the magpie and the myriad bellbird calls from the surrounding forest.

Patsy asked, "Please, please, Miss Jenkins, do tell me what the surprise is?"

Clara released a little giggle before replying, "It wouldn't be a surprise if I tell you."

"Is it a new book?" Patsy's question was punctuated by a nearby whipbird.

The broad grin expanding across Clara's face gave her away as she turned to face Patsy.

Infected by the contagion of Clara's smile, Patsy stopped walking and clapped her hands together. "I knew it! Please, just tell me what it is." In search of some kind of clue, Patsy's eyes darted around the woven wicker picnic hamper her tutor carried. "Is it about physics?" She jumped the next two steps and adopted a quicker stride than before to try and catch up to Clara who was now several paces ahead.

Clara raised a finger, a symbol of partial surrender to Patsy's wishes. "Ah, now that's something I am prepared to answer." She slowed her descent down the pathway so Patsy could catch up. "No, it's not about physics. It's more to do with biology."

Patsy came to an abrupt halt. Her eyes cast downward as far as they could go. "Biology? I thought it might be something exciting."

Clara's smile faded and she raised a hand to her brow as she took a deep breath to help compose herself. *It's okay, Clara. After all, while she may be gifted, she is still so young. Don't expect too much of her.* She exhaled and turned her attention back to Patsy, then placed a hand on the girl's shoulder. "Trust me, you'll be amazed." Patsy raised her eyes to look into Clara's as her tutor continued. "It's about a whole new field in science called 'Natural Selection.' It's all about how different types of animals came to be. Some scientists call it 'evolution.'"

Patsy moved past Clara and down the last few stairs that led to a small beach lining one side of the pool. She made a show of dragging her feet as she started across the sand. "How could that be as interesting as physics?"

Clara strode ahead and chose not to notice Patsy's displeasure as she took a seat on their favourite rock by the water's edge. "It's caused a lot of controversy." She pulled the book out of the hamper and handed it to Patsy. "It's called *On the Origin of Species*, and it's by a man called Charles Darwin."

Patsy took the book, but didn't look at it, preferring to continue staring at the ground. "It's a book about biology."

Clara's face screwed up in a frown. "I thought better of you than this, Patricia. We've spent almost a year together now learning about all sorts of interesting things." She stood up and walked a few paces away from her student, then turned to face her once more. Her lower lip quivered a little as she said, "This is the first time I've seen you shy away from something new."

An uneasy silence ensued.

It remained that way as Patsy sat down next to Clara on the rock, the place where they most liked to read together. After several uncomfortable seconds had passed, Patsy looked up. "Did you hear that?"

Clara looked from side to side, then said, "I don't hear anything."

"That's what I mean. The birds, the insects, they've all stopped."

The quiet was broken by a rustling sound in the bushes near the path, causing them to jump a little before turning their heads toward where they'd come from. A ginger tomcat emerged from behind and ran toward Patsy. Her face lit up as the cat approached. "Ferdinand! Do you know what's going on?"

Clara laughed as she rolled her eyes skyward. "Oh, but wouldn't it be nice if he could tell you."

Ferdinand purred and rubbed himself against Patsy as she stroked the back of his neck. "He used to tell me all sorts of things." She turned her focus back to Clara. "But he keeps his thoughts to himself these days."

Clara watched while Ferdinand looked at Patsy and let out a big meow. Then the cat turned toward the pool. "You know what? I think he actually is trying to tell you something, like he wants you to look at the water."

They both shifted their gaze toward the pool as a swirling vortex began stirring in its centre. Seeing Clara's wide-eyed expression, Patsy placed a hand on the woman's knee. "It's okay, Miss Jenkins, this happened last year, and the year before that."

Clara was speechless as she stood and took Patsy's hand in hers. "I think we should go up to the house now."

Patsy pulled her hand away as she rose to her feet and moved toward the water's edge. "You can go if you like. I want to stay and see what's coming."

"Coming? What do mean by coming?" asked Clara.

"It's a long story, and we usually keep it a secret. But I trust that you won't tell anybody about it."

The air above the pond began spinning, creating a whistling noise that held their attention on the vortex. It had grown wider, creating a hollow in its centre, a hollow that started moving toward the shore. There was something Patsy could see within its core. It was hard to focus on it at first, but as it came closer, it became clearer. The face of a boy.

Clara said, "I can't believe I'm seeing this. It must be a dream."

Patsy looked back over her shoulder to where Clara still stood, her arms wrapped tight about her chest. "It's okay, Miss Jenkins, I've witnessed this before. I can assure you it's quite real."

"That doesn't make me feel any better about it."

The vortex spread wider, allowing the boy to be seen from head to toe.

He was lanky, with dark wavy hair and freckles on his cheeks. It looked to Patsy that he was around fourteen or fifteen years of age. He was staring at a small metal rectangular object that he held in his right hand. As far as Patsy could tell, he seemed to be talking to it. And his clothes, they were so unusual. He wore a shirt that had no collar or buttons. But most bizarre of all, it had a colourful picture on it of a screaming man with long hair holding what looked to be a disfigured violin against his waist. A strange kind of knapsack was on his back, and he wore blue trousers. As he came closer, she looked at his shoes. They were like no shoes she'd seen before, made of the brightest coloured fabric Patsy had ever seen. He lowered his small metal box then looked up at Patsy and said, "You must be Patsy. Patsy McIntyre." He glanced across at Clara. "And you must be her tutor, Clara Jenkins."

Clara swallowed hard, took a deep breath, and found the courage to step forward. She placed her hands on her hips and asked, "Who are you?" She took another step forward. "And how do you know our names?"

The boy's face lit up when he looked at the book Patsy was holding. "Oh wow! An original edition of Darwin."

"Answer me!" demanded Clara, her jaw trembling as she leaned forward. Her breathing had become short and loud.

The boy raised his eyebrows and leaned back in response to Clara's act of defiance. He recomposed himself, then stepped up to the riverbank and extended his hand. "Oh, sorry. I'm Jai, Jai Williams. I'm Patsy's great-great-great-great-grandson."

Clara ignored his gesture. "That's preposterous."

With Jai having cleared the water, the vortex had subsided. There was no sign of moisture anywhere on him or his strange clothing. Patsy giggled. "What a curious name you've got. It's almost as strange and funny as your clothes."

Clara spoke through clenched teeth. "Answer me." Her hands had screwed up into such tight fists that her nails were cutting into her palms. "How do you know our names?"

Jai smiled at Patsy then looked toward Clara. "How could I not?" He extended his arms as though the answer should be obvious. "You two are legends!"

Before Clara could reply, Colin's voice rang out from the top of the path. "Drop whatever you're holding and move away from my daughter."

Jai looked up and saw Colin's silhouette, the barrel of a flintlock directed toward him. Without taking his eyes off Colin he lowered the rectangular box to the ground, raised his hands above his head, and took two paces away from Patsy and Clara before asking, "Are you Colin McIntyre?"

"I'll be asking the questions. Why are you here?"

"Your ancestors, my mother and grandmother, they sent me to seek your help."

Colin began working his way down the steps, the flintlock still fixed on the boy. "What kind of help?"

"My little sister and the Book of Wisdom—" Jai struggled to get the words out as a tear ran down his cheek. "They've been taken." He wiped the tear away with the back of his hand. "The Nasqa, they took both of them."

*

Sean O'Malley left the chapel and took a deep breath. It was the first time he'd been in control of such a simple function in as long as he could remember. No more feeling like a passenger in his own body. Now, he was free of the Nasqa, free of the thief that had stolen his body and soul, using his mind the way a puppeteer uses strings. He pulled Governor Pritchard's letter of recommendation from his pocket. The very presence of the letter made him wonder if his freedom was an illusion. He looked down Macquarie Street toward Circular Quay and the Rocks. The undertakers the Governor had referred him to were located in Argyle Street. There were plenty of pubs between where he stood and his destination. Sean couldn't help but think that was part of the governor's reckoning. He reached into his pocket and pulled out his purse. He peered inside at the five gold sovereigns and ten shillings.

He was now the one in control.

No publican was going to get their hands on this accidental wealth.

He turned toward Hyde Park and looked to the distant spires of Saint Mary's Cathedral.

Confession, that's what he needed.

Sean started walking south toward the cathedral, determined to cleanse his soul of the corruption that had been so entrenched while the Nasqa had controlled him.

He looked around as he made his way along the busy thoroughfare, bumping into passers-by and offering cheerful apologies on each occasion. "Begging your pardon, sir." "My humblest apologies." "Sorry, sir. I'll try to take care to watch where I'm going."

On reaching the stairs to the cathedral he straightened his jacket and tried to appear taller. He couldn't remember the last time he'd ventured into a church. This would be the beginning of a new path for him, the path of righteousness. Maybe I'd have taken vows had that dreadful thing not taken control of my mind.

The scale of the building took his breath away. As he passed from the hot sun into its welcoming shelter, the aromas of soot and incense replaced the smell of the street in his nostrils. He glanced to his right and noticed a marble font containing what he assumed to be holy water. He dipped his fingertips in, then crossed himself before he made his way toward the altar, all the while marvelling at how the sunlight danced in the stained-glass window that dominated the towering back wall.

"Bless you, my son."

Sean turned and saw a priest wearing a black robe. There was a purple sash around his waist, and he wore a skull cap of the same colour. The priest looked to be in his sixties and wore a ring characterised by a large ruby. "Good morning, Your Holiness, sir. I've come looking to make a confession."

The priest raised an eyebrow. "Well, you timed it well. I was just making my way to the confessional." He gestured toward a group of three doors to the left of the cathedral. "Come, you can be the first to repent your sins."

Sean knelt in the dark confessional and waited for the priest to open the panel that would allow him to confess all that had happened. After what seemed an eternity, the wooden panel slid across. The priest on the other side of the heavy wire mesh seemed oblivious to his existence. Sean O'Malley initially fumbled with his words. "Bless me, Your Holiness, sir, for I am a sinner. That is to say, bless me, Father, for I have sinned. It is, by my reckoning, so many years since my last confession that I've now lost count."

"The Lord is forgiving of sins to those who repent, my son, regardless of how many years it may have been between confessions."

"There are a great many terrible things that I have done, but all of them occurred while I was possessed by evil."

"As long as you confess in full the Lord will forgive you."

"Well then, perhaps I should start with what I think the Lord would take the greatest affront to. That'd be the terrible things I've done to a man of the cloth."

"Did this man of God have a name that you knew of?"

"Oh, yes, Your Holiness. They call him the Reverend Alfred Casey. A man who fights evil like no other man I know."

The priest looked up at Sean for the first time. "I'd like to know about this priest, and how he fights evil. I'd like to know all that you can tell me."

.

Felibrey looked around, stunned by the enormous and diverse range of goods on the multitude of shelves. He stood silhouetted in the doorway of the Blackheath General Store. Specks of dust danced in the golden morning sunlight that streamed in through the shopfront's windows. Entering the shop, he tried to ignore the sensory overload of the new experience and focused instead on his goal of approaching the main counter. Once he'd reached his destination, Felibrey turned his eyes to meet those of the shop's attendant, a man in his sixties with bushes of white hair where he wasn't already balding. He had a meticulously waxed moustache and large sideburns. A stretch of silver chain revealed that he had a fob watch in the left pocket of his simple, grey waistcoat. Felibrey pulled a small purse from the pocket of his trousers as he said, "Hello."

The attendant placed his hands on the counter and leaned forward. He looked deep into Felibrey's eyes. "And good day to you, sir." He twisted his head a little and raised an eyebrow as he studied his customer's face. "I don't recall that I've seen you in here before."

Felibrey released an awkward smile. "This is the first time I've been to a shop. The Reverend Casey said that if I give you some coins, in exchange you'll give me the building materials I need. He said that you're a man who can be trusted."

"Aye, that's how it generally works. Tell me, what would your name be? I like to be aware of who I'm dealing with."

"My name is Felibrey."

"Well, Mr. Felibrey, I'm pleased to make your acquaintance." He extended a hand toward the Reverend's disciple. "My name is Lord, Jonathan Lord, but you're welcome to call me Jon. What would be your Christian name?"

Felibrey felt unsure how to respond. He stood with his mouth open but was unable to find any words.

"That's okay, Mr. Felibrey. I've met people before who are shy about such things on first meeting someone. I cannot help but wonder though, how does it come to pass that someone of your age has never before visited a general store?"

"I come from far away."

Jon nodded in acknowledgment. "That would explain the accent. You speak the language well, considering."

Felibrey smiled. "The Reverend is a good teacher."

"Aye, he's a good man in general. I'm guessing you'd be one of the twelve immigrants who offered to help him rebuild his house?"

"Yes, that's correct."

"So, did you come from the goldfields?"

"No, I come from far away. I have no interest in gold."

"Well, Mr. Felibrey, I must say, I like a man who'll travel a good distance to help another, especially one who has little interest in gold. What exactly would you be needing? Is it for the Reverend's house?"

"No, his house is finished. It's for the cottage I'm building for my fiancé and myself." Felibrey pulled a piece of paper from his pocket. "I have a list."

*

"Why should we believe you?" asked Colin, still pointing his flintlock at Jai.

The boy stood with his hands raised. He looked at his rectangular box then back to Colin. "I have pictures, photographs on my phone that will prove it."

"Phone?" Colin looked to Clara, who shrugged her shoulders.

"That's what the box you asked me to put down is called. It has lots of photographs in it, and other things as well." Jai bent his knees and started lowering his arms to reach for the phone.

"Get your hands back up. I've no desire to shoot a mere boy, but so help me, if you don't do as I say, then I'll have little choice." Colin glanced across to Patsy. "Patricia, would you be so kind as to retrieve our friend's little box, his 'phone' as he calls it?"

Patsy darted across and retrieved the phone from the ground and then raced back to be by Clara's side. They inspected it together, turning it over and looking for how they might open the box. Clara looked at Jai. "How do we open it?"

Jai kept his eyes on Colin and the barrel of the flintlock. "You don't open it. You just need to wake it from sleep mode then open the gallery app."

Clara raised her voice. "That makes no sense at all. Are you trying to make fun of us?"

Patsy took the phone from Clara. "Maybe I can open it. I've always been good at puzzles."

Jai said, "I can take you through it step by step. But you have to promise that you won't drop it when the screen lights up."

"My daughter doesn't have to promise you anything." Colin was working his way down the pathway, one measured step at a time.

"Please, Mr. McIntyre. It cost a lot of money. Mum will kill me if I go back with a cracked screen on it."

Patsy turned the phone over. "I don't see anything that looks like a screen."

"The side that's black, that's the screen," said Jai.

"It's so smooth. It's like black glass." Patsy stared at her reflection and ran a finger from top to bottom of the screen.

"There's a small button just below where your finger is. You need to press that, just gently."

Clara put a hand on Patsy's shoulder. "I have a pencil with me. Perhaps we should place this 'phone' of his on the rock and use that to press the button in case there's something spring-loaded inside."

Patsy ignored Clara's advice and pressed the button. "Arrh!!" Patsy and Clara screamed out in unison. Startled by the brightness of the screen lighting up after she'd pressed the button, Patsy threw the phone onto the sand.

Jai's face contorted as he cried out, "My phone!"

Colin raised the flintlock and pointed the sights toward the phone. "What kind of magic is in that box?"

With the rifle now pointed at something other than his face, Jai felt comfortable to lower his hands a little. "It's not magic, sir. It's technology, electronics, a type of science. Can I show you how it works?"

Patsy folded her arms and cocked her head to one side. "All magic is really just science. People only call it magic when they don't understand the science behind it."

Colin closed his eyes for a moment and grimaced. Why must she be so like her grandmother?

Patsy squatted down to pick up the phone, forcing her father to lower the rifle. "Patricia, what in God's name do you think you're doing?"

Patsy ignored him as she inspected the device. "Look, the glass is a bright blue, with little symbols inside coloured squares." She pointed it toward her father. "See?"

"Patricia, we can't know if it's safe. I want you to put it down now, or so help me there'll be hell to pay."

A voice called out from above them on the pathway. "Have you gone mad?"

Great, thought Colin, *just what we didn't need right now*. He turned around to face Patsy's grandmother, Neridah, as she came down the path wearing a green velvet dress with an elaborate white embroidered collar. Her mop of thick dark hair fell about her shoulders in a manner that suggested it had yet to be brushed since she'd woken. Colin set out to reply. "I—"

"Why are you waving that thing about in front of your daughter?"

Colin gestured toward Jai. "I was—"

Noticing the phone Patsy was holding and ignoring Colin, Neridah commented, "Oh, that looks interesting."

"It's his," said Patsy as she pointed at Jai.

Neridah looked at Jai and smiled. "Hello. My, what strange clothes you're wearing."

"He claims to be from the future," said Clara. She turned toward the pool. "He came out of there, and he's not even wet."

Neridah looked at Clara. "Well, if he says he's from the future, then I guess he probably is."

Clara held her hands against her cheeks as she shook her head. "No, he can't be. That's impossible."

"His coming from the future doesn't dictate that we should trust him," said Colin.

Clara stared at Colin. Her eyes suggested she was shocked that he could be entertaining the possibility that Jai had been telling the truth.

Neridah looked at Colin's flintlock, then to his face. "It doesn't mean you should be pointing that gun at him either, especially not when Patricia's already here." Clara's expression betrayed her continuing bewilderment at what she was hearing. "I mean really, Colin. Why even bother with your gun when it's so useless compared to what your daughter's capable of?"

"Do you really think it's wise to have this discussion in front of Miss Jenkins?" replied Colin.

Neridah shrugged her shoulders. "Um, begging your pardon, but didn't she just see someone come through the portal? Don't you think the cat's out of the bag now?"

"Could you please not talk about me as though I'm not here?" asked Clara.

Colin and Neridah both looked at Clara, then to each other, before realising that Patsy and Jai were standing together looking at his phone. Patsy looked up and said, "Jai just showed me how it works." She held up the phone so the screen was facing her father and grandmother. "Look, this is a photograph of his mother."

Neridah and Colin stepped closer to confirm what they were seeing. Colin turned to Neridah. "She looks just like you, only with red hair."

Neridah looked at Jai, then back to the photograph. She looked at Jai again. The colour drained out of her face as though she'd seen a ghost. "It can't be," she whispered. "You look just like—"

Clara said, "Could someone please have the courtesy to explain what's going on?"

Colin looked at Patsy. "Perhaps you should take Miss Jenkins up to have a chat to your mother, and then you can go and ask Darcy if we might be able to borrow some clothing from him so we can dress our new friend in a way that won't disturb Cook and the other servants too much." He turned to Jai. "And you, young man, might want to explain yourself in more detail while we wait for Patricia to return."

CHAPTER 2

Jai stepped out of Darcy's bedroom and into the living area of the servants' quarters. With Darcy close behind, the boy paraded in front of Patsy and Neridah. He spread his arms out and asked, "Well, what do you reckon?" The trousers were baggy, but far too short for someone of Jai's height. Despite that, their looseness around his waist made it clear that, without the bulky suspenders, they'd soon be around his ankles. The shirt was much wider across the shoulders than Jai's frame, and even with the top button done up, it hung loose around his neck.

Patsy covered her mouth to hide a giggle, then Neridah raised her chin as she said, "You look far more presentable."

Darcy stepped forward and said, "Aye, but there's still one thing missing." He took off his flat cap and put it on Jai's head, pulling it down at the front as much as he could so Jai's eyes were hidden from view. He smirked as he turned to Patsy and Neridah. "We need to show mercy to the public at large and hide his face as best we can."

While everyone else in the room was laughing at his expense, Jai lifted the front of the cap, then turned to Darcy and asked, "What will you wear?"

"I've got another just like it… but I'd happily walk around with the sun in my eyes for a few days if that's the price of protecting the people from seeing too much of your face."

Jai smiled. "That's all well and good, but if you care that much, maybe you should stay indoors yourself."

Patsy said, "To be honest, your other clothes were a better fit, but at least you won't scare Cook now."

Darcy looked at her out of the corner of his eye. "Would you be sure of that? I've seen Cook jump at the sight of her own shadow."

"I've seen her jump at less than that!"

"Patricia!" Neridah glared at her granddaughter. "After everything that Cook has been through, don't you think she deserves more respect than that?"

Patsy cast her eyes down. "I'm sorry…" She glanced up at Darcy. He pulled a face and Patsy couldn't help but grin. She looked once more at Neridah's serious expression and burst out laughing. "I'm sorry, Nana-Neri, I just can't take you seriously when you're angry."

A subtle smile appeared on Neridah's face as she shook her head and stood up. "You most certainly are my granddaughter. I'd best go now and rescue your mother from Miss Jenkin's frantic questioning."

Patsy cast her eyes toward the ceiling and sighed. "I do hope she's alright. She was so distressed before."

Darcy said, "If you'd be asking me, I think it's about time she knew the truth about you lot."

Neridah glared at him then made her way to the front door, calling out as she went. "Well, Jai, all I can say is that I hope you've better manners than our friend Darcy."

Jai looked at Darcy. The Irish lad pulled a face as he shrugged his shoulders.

Patsy stood up and gestured to Jai. "Come on, I'll take you for a walk around the property."

*

Mrs Gladys Taylor stared at her new husband as their sulky approached the gate of Springwood Barracks. "Who'd have thought it, huh?" She turned her attention to her wedding band, twisting it as she spoke. "That you and I would end up hitched?"

Captain Taylor closed his eyes and grimaced. "I could really do without the reminder."

Gladys looked toward the barracks, then back to the Captain. "When we go in there, the men will expect us to behave like newlyweds."

The Captain stared straight ahead, refusing to answer.

"Don't worry yourself too much. I think I'll be more comfortable with the company of a bottle of rum than your good self anyway."

Captain Taylor turned to Gladys. "As much as it pains me to say it, that is completely unacceptable. I may be appalled by your presence, but the fact is, you are now my wife, and I will not tolerate any such behaviour, as I'm sure your host wouldn't either."

"Hah! What's she going to do about it? Be a nagging little voice in the back of my head? It only takes a few drinks to drown that out."

"Need I remind you that, as well as being my wife, you are the Governor's representative for education standards. How can you hope to muster the respect of the Blue Mountains community if you're falling around drunk in the mud? You need to tap into your host's experience if you want to pull this off."

A voice called out, "Congratulations, Captain." Captain Taylor and his bride turned to see where the voice had come from. A young lieutenant was running up to them. "Can I take your bags for you, sir?"

Captain Taylor brought the sulky to a halt. "Yes, of course."

The lieutenant looked at Gladys. "Welcome to Springwood Barracks, Mrs Taylor. We'll do our best to make you welcome."

Gladys cast a dismissive glance his way. "It's got to be better than the last time I was here."

"Excuse me, ma'am, when might that have been?"

Captain Taylor glared at his wife. "I think that she's referencing a visit to another barracks in Sydney. I don't believe she realises how different they can be."

An uncomfortable silence ensued as the three walked to the Captain's quarters. Once their bags were inside, the lieutenant said, "I'll be seeing you both in the mess hall for dinner then."

"Yes, quite." Captain Taylor closed the door as the lieutenant left the room. He turned and saw Gladys holding up an empty jar.

"We've got a problem."

"What do you mean, we've got a problem?"

"It's escaped."

Silence.

"The stringworm. It's managed to do a jump out of its jar."

"You must be joking."

"Trust me, I wouldn't joke about something like that."

"How? Isn't the lid still on?"

"You need more than a sealed jar to contain these things when they can smell something like that portal at the McIntyres'. That's the sort of place where they like to feed."

"But that's half a day's ride from here."

Gladys shook her head. "Well, it's gone, and that's the only thing that makes sense."

Captain Taylor stabbed a finger into his wife's chest. "Well, you, my dear, can be the one who tells Pritchard."

*

Patsy gestured toward the garden shed. "I've found all sorts of wonderful things in that shed, but Father gets quite cross if he knows I've been in there without his permission."

Jai glanced at the shed then turned to Patsy as they continued down the paddock. "I'm surprised I haven't met Reverend Casey yet."

Patsy laughed. "Why's that? It's not like he lives here."

"But I thought…" Jai let his words hang in mid-air.

Patsy stopped walking. "Oh, so is there something the boy from the future knows that I don't?" She spun around in a circle as though dancing. "Nana-Neri gets very angry with him sometimes." She paused and glanced up to the treetops. "Well, quite often really. She spends all week talking about how much she misses her Alfred"—she held her hands to her chest in a mocking fashion—"and how she's so looking forward to seeing him again." She spread her arms out. "Then, when he comes for dinner on the weekend, she almost always ends up arguing with him and storming off to her room in tears."

"Wow, I'm sorry to hear that. I just thought—"

Patsy cut him off and pointed to the bottom of the paddock. "Can you see that?"

"See what?"

"See how the trees look different there?"

"Oh yeah, and the light looks different too… more golden."

Patsy's face betrayed her excitement. "Krinkle-myst!"

Jai stared at her. "What do you mean?"

"Krinkle-myst, he's a wood-elf."

"My grandmother's told me stories about the legend of Krinkle-myst for as long as I can remember. But it's just stories."

Patsy gestured toward the shimmering portal leading to the forest that played host to Krinkle-myst's cabin. "That pathway, it only appears when he's here."

"Are you telling me he's real?"

Patsy picked up the hem of her dress and started running. "Of course he's real. Come on, he's probably here because of you."

Jai shook his head then started running after her. Once through the portal, he came to a standstill and turned around. "I can't see the house anymore."

Realising he wasn't following anymore, Patsy stopped as well. "Of course not, silly. We've passed through to another world."

"Oh yeah? And what world is this then?"

"Krinkle-myst says it's the world that no one's ever seen."

"Never heard of that one before. So, where is this Krinkle-myst?"

"He'll be in his cabin, working on one of his fairy tales."

"And how do we find his cabin?"

"By allowing ourselves to be there."

"By what?"

Patsy sighed. "For someone who's descended from a long line of witches, you don't seem to understand magic very well."

"You're still not making any sense."

Patsy looked up. "Or we could fly there."

"Fly?"

"You've never flown anywhere?"

"I've been on a plane and flown to Bali."

Patsy screwed up her face. "What's a plane?"

Jai smiled. "Planes are amazing. They're marvels of modern engineering."

Patsy stared at him.

"I guess that doesn't tell you much." He looked up for a moment and pondered how to explain a plane to someone who'd never even imagined such a thing before. "You know how a horse and carriage can carry people from one place to another?"

"Yes."

"Well, imagine a really big carriage, one that can carry hundreds of people and that flies through the air."

Patsy frowned at him.

"Seriously, I'm not making it up."

"How do they fly?"

"They have wings, like a bird, and really big engines."

"That sounds ridiculous."

"It's true."

"I'm going to get angry if you keep making fun of me."

"Seriously, I'm not lying."

"You wouldn't like it if I get angry."

"But I'm telling the truth." Jai could sense that she wasn't joking. He pulled his phone out of his pocket. "I think I might have a photo—"

A broad smile spread across Patsy's face as she looked past Jai's shoulder. "Pixie-dust!"

Jai turned around and saw the dancing ball of sparkles. "Oh, wow!"

"That's how we'll find Krinkle-myst's cabin. We'll follow the pixie-dust."

Jai tried to reach out and touch it, but it evaded his hand at every attempt, as though it were teasing him. Then it shot up high and started heading down the path.

"Come on, let's go." Patsy pushed herself up from the ground and was airborne in an instant. She moved about as though treading water in the air while waiting for Jai to do the same.

"What the... how'd you do that?"

"It's not so much that you do it, it's more that you let it happen." She reached down and took his hand. "Come on, just push off the ground."

Jai pulled his hand away. "No, I can't."

"If you want to be like that, then good luck keeping up." Patsy did a frog kick with her legs then started making sweeping actions with her arms to move through the air in the direction of the pixie-dust. Within seconds she had already travelled twenty paces.

Jai started running. "Wait! I can't keep up!"

Patsy was already out of sight up ahead. Her voice seemed distant. "Of course you can."

Jai kept putting one leg in front of the other, running faster than he ever had before. "I'll get lost out here."

Patsy's voice was barely audible. "Then you'd better keep up."

As he rounded a bend, Jai noticed a large tree trunk had fallen across the path. He was moving too fast to stop, so had little choice but to try and jump over it. He jumped high enough that his feet landed on the top of the log, then he pushed up and forward, determined to catch up to Patsy. He moved his arms as he'd seen Patsy move hers, hoping he might gain extra distance from his leap. The ground was moving rapidly beneath him, and yet he seemed to be maintaining his height. Then he noticed the ground coming closer. He moved his arms again and imagined himself in the pool at his school's swimming carnival. He kicked with his feet and brought one arm at a time over his shoulder, as though swimming freestyle. Faster and faster, he stroked, not thinking of where he was, just the need to catch up to Patsy.

"Come on, the pixie-dust is way ahead of us now."

Jai could see Patsy up ahead now, and the treetops far below. "I can't believe it! I'm flying!"

"I don't really see it as flying. I think of it more as another kind of swimming."

"This is amazing!"

"Not as amazing as you expecting me to believe hundreds of people can fly in a box."

"But they do."

Patsy ignored him then pointed to a narrow stream of smoke up ahead. "That'll be from Krinkle-myst's chimney." She pushed against the air in front of her to slow herself down. Jai followed suit and started descending. "It's a lot quicker if you just allow yourself to follow the pixie-dust, but I could tell you weren't ready to try that yet."

Jai was looking below him at the approaching forest floor as he moved his legs as though pedalling a bicycle. "I can't believe how much this is like being in water."

"Air and water are very much the same as each other, you know. People just assume that because water is denser than air, that they can float in one but not the other. Anyone can swim through the air if they know how."

Once they landed, Jai's knees felt weak and he collapsed to the ground. "Whoa! I feel like I've run a marathon."

Patsy gave a reassuring smile as she offered a hand and helped him to his feet. "It's a bit like that the first time. It takes a bit more energy than swimming in water, but you move a lot faster."

Jai turned to face the little stone cabin. "There's no windows or doors, and it looks way too small for us to fit inside of it."

"It doesn't need doors or windows. Here, take my hand. Close your eyes and imagine you're inside. Allow yourself to be inside."

Jai did as she suggested, then heard the crackling of an open fire. He opened his eyes and looked at the room around them. There were two wooden chairs by the fire. A large cast iron pot was suspended from a tripod holding it over the flames. The steam rising from the pot carried aromas of cloves, mint and cinnamon. He turned to scan the rest of the room, finding it to be empty other than a small writing desk in the far corner. And sitting at that desk was a wood-elf, who wouldn't have been much taller than the height of Jai's knee.

Patsy ran toward the desk. "Krinkle-myst!"

Krinkle-myst turned and glanced over the top of his glasses. "Hello. You took your time getting here."

Patsy squatted low when she'd reached the desk, trying to bring her head down to Krinkle-myst's eye level. "I know. Jai's not used to allowing himself to move from one place to another."

Krinkle-myst glanced past Patsy to the nervous teenager standing near the fire. "Hmmph! Why does that not surprise me?" He pointed an accusing finger in Jai's direction. "There seems to be quite a few areas where you're lacking in wisdom, young man."

Jai opened his mouth to speak, but found himself lost for words when he noticed that he was now sitting in one of the chairs, with Patsy in the other. Krinkle-myst was standing by the fire, using a ladle to fill a metal cup with the sweet-smelling brew. He handed the cup to Jai. "Here, this will warm your soul and make you more comfortable."

As Jai wrapped a hand around the warm cup, he asked, "What is it?"

A smile filled the wood-elf's face as he looked up. "It's Mrs Krinkle-myst's special heart-warming recipe, perfected over thousands of millennia."

Jai took a sip. A warm glow embraced his taste buds, then spread through his mouth, oozing out to his cheeks before enveloping every part of his being with a sense of contentment. "Oh, wow. This is amazing." Krinkle-myst handed another cup of the elixir to Patsy. After she'd tried it, Jai could tell from her expression that it was having the same impact on her. He turned back to the wood-elf and whispered, "I feel so privileged."

"And so you should," Krinkle-myst snapped back at him.

Jai leaned back in his chair as Krinkle-myst stepped closer to him.

"Do you have any idea how much trouble you've caused me today?"

Jai held up his free hand in a look of surrender. He opened his mouth, but no words came out.

"As if one timeline isn't enough to look after! I was just about ready for Mrs Krinkle-myst and I to go on a holiday to one of the most beautiful places that no one's ever seen. Then along comes Jai, happily prancing his way through time and creating a whole new timeline for me to have to deal with."

"I, I didn't know."

"Then why'd you do it?"

"My little sister, and the Book of Wisdom. The Nasqa—"

"Yes, yes, I know all that already. I want to know what made you think that travelling through time might make things any better."

Jai looked across at Patsy. "All my life, my mother and grandmother have talked about the legendary Patsy McIntyre, and how no problem was ever too big to—"

Krinkle-myst reached across and covered Jai's mouth. "Now, just hold it right there. You don't want to make this worse by telling Patsy details about her future." He pulled his hand away and shook his head while holding a hand against his forehead. "Why? Why is it that nobody seems to understand time travel?"

Patsy said, "I remember when Kerridwen came, and the trouble that the time freezes—"

Krinkle-myst waved a hand at her dismissively. "Yes, yes, but that was just time freezes." He pointed at Jai. "This young man travelled over one hundred and fifty years through time."

Jai said, "But my grandmother had read about how to do that in the Book of Wisdom. Surely if it's in there, then there must be times when it's okay to do it."

"And you consider yourself a sound judge of when it's the right time to make such a choice?" asked Krinkle-myst.

"Look, I'm sorry. Okay?"

"No, it's not okay."

Patsy stood up and stamped a foot, causing a rumble to shake through the building. Jai and Krinkle-myst froze in response. Patsy took a step toward them. "We get it. Jai shouldn't have come here. But he's here. Is getting angry really going to help anything?"

Krinkle-myst sat in a small chair that had appeared behind him. "No, I guess not."

"I don't understand. You've always been so calm and measured in the past," Patsy said.

"I know. It's been a hard day." Krinkle-myst looked at Jai. "Have another sip on that elixir and I'll tell you a bit about time. You see, most people think of time from totally the wrong perspective. They see it in a linear fashion, believing the only thing that's real is the moment. That the past is fixed solid in history, and that the future is flexible." They had now transported to Krinkle-myst's writing desk, where he was drawing a line across a page. "They perceive time in a two-dimensional manner and as something that moves in one direction." When he'd finished drawing the line, they were back by the fire, with Krinkle-myst holding up the sheet of paper. He held it so the sheet faced Patsy and Jai. "This is how most people view time." He then turned the page, so they were looking down the length of the line. "But the correct way to view time is like this, with all points co-existing together. There is little relevance as to what is future or past unless you are sitting somewhere within that line. From outside the line, it's all one and the same moment."

Jai was focusing on the sheet Krinkle-myst was holding. "I'm really struggling to get my head around this."

"Of course you are. Anyone silly enough to use a portal to travel through time would struggle. Now, imagine that you are somewhere on this timeline, not knowing that everything that ever has happened, or ever will happen, is already defined. If you look back, what do you see?"

Jai looked at Patsy for reassurance before answering. She gave him a polite nod of encouragement. "Memories?"

Krinkle-myst smiled. "Exactly! But you can only see back so far. And the further back you look, the more those memories blur into those of parallel timelines, causing them to become distorted and inaccurate."

"So, if there's already multiple timelines, why should it be a problem if I've created another one?"

"Because you've created it using brute force rather than nature's way of just allowing them to unfurl, like a flower opening in spring. It's as though you've driven a bulldozer through a hundred and fifty years of past and future memories."

Patsy asked, "What do you mean by future memories?"

"I was wondering when someone would ask that one. The future is no different to the past, it's already happened. And the past is just as flexible as people perceive the future to be. Most people lack the comprehension, or even the ability, to see their future memories as clearly as they see their past. But there are some who do see them just as clearly."

"Clairvoyants?" asked Jai.

Krinkle-myst snapped a finger and pointed to Jai. "Now, I'm starting to think you might have promise. Yes! And there're others too." He looked toward Patsy. "The more powerful of the Crossworld Witches have always shown somewhat of a flair for seeing the future memories. But you have to be aware that, like with past memories, future memories are distorted by the parallel timelines."

Jai took another sip on his elixir, then asked, "These parallel timelines, are they related to the multiverse?"

Krinkle-myst smiled. "And...?"

"Well, they're all sort of connected, by strings of energy that pass through all of them... or something like that," said Jai.

"Yes, and that's important. Those strings create pathways through space, time, and different realities, different crossworlds. Most of the time, if someone uses a portal like the one on the McIntyre property, there is a magnetic repulsion that ensures one doesn't cross into a world that is close to the one you're already in. But there are other ways to pass through the Crossworlds that are more subtle. Sometimes, just being sad enough about an event in your past will actually shift you into a version of reality where whatever it was that happened was worse than it really was."

Patsy was getting more interested in the conversation now. "But if someone slips into another nearby crossworld like that, wouldn't they end up facing themselves?"

Krinkle-myst shook his head. "No, they effectively swap realities, so for the one in the world that is a sadder version of reality, they suddenly find things looking more positive. There's a blurring of realities for most people where they are able to drift from one reality to another. Sometimes it's driven by positive feelings, and sometimes by more negative ones." Krinkle-myst poured himself a cup of the elixir. "The problem we have now is that you, young man, have travelled into your past on the wrong timeline. Your reality is not the future of this Patricia McIntyre. You're interfering in the wrong timeline."

Jai and Patsy looked at each other, then Patsy turned to Krinkle-myst. "So, does that mean we're not related?"

Krinkle-myst looked upwards and shook his head before replying. "Of course you're still related. Relationships carry across timelines. If he were far enough removed that he were in a wholly different crossworld, then the connection becomes separate. But as it stands, he comes from what is a possible future for you, albeit an unlikely one." He turned to Jai. "And you've now effectively altered your past in a manner that's severed every timeline you've crossed and created whole new branches with unpredictable outcomes. Some of which will likely spread into this reality. These tears in the fabric of reality are hard to stop when they start to spread. They're like an infectious disease."

Lost for words, Jai buried his head in his hands.

Patsy looked at the wood-elf and said, "He was only trying to help his sister."

"The most calamitous events always start with the most noble of intentions."

"Is there anything we can do to fix it?"

"Not unless you're able to find your way to Jai's timeline and stop him from coming back."

Patsy stood up. "Come on Jai, let's go."

"Go where?" asked Jai.

Her eyes were narrow and focused as she glared at the wood-elf. "I'm going to consult the Book of Wisdom and find a way back to your timeline."

Krinkle-myst smiled and slapped his knee. "Now that's the Patsy McIntyre I'm used to."

In the next instant, Krinkle-myst had vanished.

⁎

Archbishop Darvos threw down his brandy then asked the Governor, "How'd you know the gravedigger would come to the cathedral? Hadn't you directed him to seek employment?"

Governor Pritchard smiled as he leaned back in his chair. "Come now, haven't you inhabited your host long enough to get a grip on how these creatures' minds work? This world has two types of hosts. There are those like Gladys, who long for the power we afford them, and the foolish ones who hanker for freedom, the ones who want to 'cleanse' themselves of us. As if the gravedigger was going to do as I'd asked after he'd been set free. Particularly when he'd just received more money than the poor wretch had ever seen in his miserable life."

"Well, I'm glad you warned me he was coming."

"So, you understand the problem now that he's confessed?"

"Oh, yes. This Reverend Casey, he needs to be dealt with sooner rather than later. I'll be heading straight to the railway station from here. We can't afford to have rogues like him out there when we've put so much effort into taking control of the churches in this country."

"I always knew you were the right choice to take over the bishop."

"Yes, but it's a shame about the arthritic knee in this body."

"Well, my friend, once you've dealt with our little problem, you can feel free to choose whatever host you please."

•

"Patricia!" Meredith was calling to her daughter as she walked down the paddock. She decided it would be prudent to check the garden shed before heading down the pathway to the pool in the creek. As she approached the wooden structure, she noticed the shimmer of golden light glowing at the edge of the bush, the portal to the forest that was home to Krinkle-myst's cabin.

Her pace slowed as she approached the portal, twisting her head as though it may help her see more of it. As it grew larger, she marvelled at how different the trees looked on the other side. Its shimmering light had her mesmerised. This was the first time she'd seen the path since her mother and Patsy had used it to hide from the soldiers a year ago. It was as though she could hear a song within the dancing sunbeams. The spell was broken when Patsy came racing through it, with Jai close behind. The boy tripped on the edge of the portal, bringing Patsy to the ground with him as he tumbled forward. The two of them looked at each other, then burst out laughing.

"Patricia!"

Patsy and Jai's laughter came to an abrupt halt when Patsy looked up and saw her mother's silhouette. It was clear from Meredith's stance that she was not impressed. Patsy looked back to Jai and couldn't help but let out a giggle.

"Patricia, this is no laughing matter."

"Sorry, Mother."

Meredith turned her attention to Jai. "And you must be the young man from the future that I've heard so much about this morning."

Jai got to his feet and offered Meredith his hand. "It's a pleasure to meet you, Mrs McIntyre."

Meredith glared at Jai's hand then looked back to Patsy. "You do recall, don't you, that the Education Department has sent a representative to Blackheath to check on how you are progressing under the tutelage of Miss Jenkins?"

Patsy rose to her feet, her eyes widening as she realised she'd forgotten all about the planned afternoon meeting. "I'm so sorry, Mother, I'd completely forgotten."

"Well, maybe you might be a little less forgetful if you actually considered asking my permission before leaping into other worlds."

Patsy sighed and lowered her head. "Sorry, Mother. It's just, I never know when the portal's going to appear. If I'd gone up to the house to let you know it was there, it may have been gone when I got back."

An uneasy silence followed. Meredith knew Patsy was right, but she certainly wasn't going to admit it. She chose to change the topic back to what was really bothering her. "The woman who's coming up from Sydney, we've been informed her name is Mrs Taylor."

Patsy replied, "Yes, I recall Miss Jenkins telling me that."

"Yes, well as it turns out, Mrs Taylor has only recently remarried. She was a widow. Her previous name was Mrs Bradshaw."

Patsy's jaw fell open.

"It gets even worse. She's now married to Captain Taylor, the man who tried to have your father hung last year. You need to lie low until she's gone, Patricia. I suggest you take Jai for a walk along the creek. She's not likely to want to look for you down there."

"But, what about Miss Jenkins, will she be alright? What if she loses her job because I'm not there?"

"She'll be fine, I'll see to that. You and Jai just need to get to the creek, and quickly. She'll be here soon, by my reckoning…"

·

Destellie rose from where she sat on the church steps, her eyes wide with excitement. She'd been there since just after sunrise when Felibrey had left. Inside the church, the Reverend Casey was up on a scaffold finishing the installation of a stained-glass window behind the altar. Destellie called out, "Reverend, he is almost here! And I could see that his cart is laid heavy with supplies. You were right."

The Reverend Alfred Casey kept his attention on the strip of window putty he was smoothing out. He checked the window was firmly in place before he turned to face Destellie. "I'm glad he's returned so soon. I felt certain he was ready for a trip into town. And far better that he does it on his own than appear too reliant on one such as myself." He climbed down the scaffold with the dexterity of a jungle primate. "Let's go out and give him the warm welcome he deserves."

Destellie ran to the door, pulling the hem of her long dress up so she could run faster. The Reverend smiled. Of all his disciples, it was Destellie who had most embraced the ways of this world. Felibrey arrived at the church entrance as she did. The Reverend's mind transported back to his teenage years as he watched them embrace, remembering the feeling of Neridah's warmth when they'd held each other close. The memory was just as fresh in his mind as it was the day it first happened. He closed his eyes and felt like he was falling as he remembered their lips coming together that day. The feelings that had overwhelmed him then had informed every decision he'd made since. He took a deep breath and whispered, "The sacrifices we make for love."

"How about you stop feeling sorry for yourself and do something about it?" The Reverend looked down at his shoulder to the pixie standing there with her arms folded.

Another voice caused him to turn the other way. "Come on, Talia, give the guy a break."

Talia pointed to Destellie and Felibrey as they remained oblivious to the rest of the world. "See that? That's what both Neridah and Alfred deserve. Forty years that poor woman spent wrapped in a cocoon in Sellemae's lair." She took to the air and hovered in front of the Reverend's nose, causing him to go cross-eyed. "What's the point in you spending all those years dedicated to rescuing her if now you deny her what these two lovebirds have?"

Bandah protested. "How many times do I have to tell you, he took a vow?"

Talia put her hands on her hips and glared at the Reverend. "Vows are made to be broken... as my husband of ten thousand years has been so deft at demonstrating."

Bandah looked away. "Not this again."

The Reverend took a step back, his brow transforming into a frown. He brushed Bandah off his shoulder, taking the pixie by surprise. "If you two don't mind, there is a happiness in this moment for two of my dear friends that I would like to share." He took a few long strides toward Felibrey and Destellie, then threw his arms around them both.

Talia stared at Bandah. "So much for that bond you were so proud of with your grundai."

Bandah shrugged his shoulders. "What can I say? That hasn't really been the same since he brought Neridah back."

"I don't understand these vows of his. Surely there's some way that he could nullify them or something."

"You'd think so, but that's not Alfred's way."

Talia shook her head. "I feel so sad for Neridah."

"I feel sad for both of them."

Talia nudged Bandah's shoulder. "Hey, do you feel like a bit of nectar? There're some really juicy flowers in a nearby crossworld. The place has a great vibe as well."

Bandah grinned. "Now you're talking my language."

They took each other's hands and vanished.

·

Patsy and Jai walked upstream. Jai kicked a stone as he said, "My mum's going to be so jealous when she finds out I met Krinkle-myst."

Patsy looked up at the boy who was staring into space. "You know what, Jai? As much as you only arrived this morning, I'm enjoying you being here. You make me happy."

Jai looked at her and let out a little laugh. "I guess that's to be expected. What, with us being related and all that. I never imagined it could be so cool to spend time with a great-great-ancestor."

"Oh, look!" Patsy pointed out a leech on a rock. Its head waved about as it tried to find the source of the blood it could smell. "We'll need to check our feet when we get back. I've often picked up a leech or two coming up to this part of the creek."

"Tell me about it. Trust me, it's just as bad in that regard a hundred and fifty years from now. Not that I've ever let a few leeches stop me." He looked around at the trees and took in a deep breath. "I've always loved it down here, and you'd be surprised how much the same it looks in the future as it does now." Jai pointed to what appeared to be another leech waving its head a metre or so ahead of them. "That's a big one."

Patsy let go of his hand and approached it. "I don't think it's a leech. It's looks somehow different."

Jai said, "It's like it's transparent."

Patsy picked up a stick and moved close to it. She crouched down and held the stick behind it. "Look, it's not really transparent, you can't see the stick behind it."

A few seconds later, the stick's image was where Patsy had expected it to be.

Jai's jaw dropped. "Time-displacement!"

Patsy turned to him and asked, "Could you please use words I understand?"

"Just watch, move the stick up again and it'll take a few seconds before its image disappears behind the leech."

Patsy moved the stick, but the image behind the transparent leech-like creature changed in ways they weren't expecting. Where they expected to see rock, they saw flower petals.

Jai put his hand on Patsy's shoulder. "This is getting freaky. And it's growing, really fast."

Before Patsy had a chance to respond, the stringworm lunged forward and expanded its sucker-like mouth to cover her left knee, the pressure of its mouth forcing the knee to bend.

"Argh!" She grabbed hold of Jai, eyes wide as she screamed, "Get it off me!"

Jai reached down and tried to grab the lips of its sucker-mouth, but his hand passed straight through it into a strange coldness. The sucker inched up Patsy's leg. She tried pushing against its mouth with her right foot, only to have the creature expand its mouth and start consuming the other leg.

Jai wrapped his arms around her shoulders. "Don't worry, I won't let you go."

Patsy's breaths were short and panicked as she reached her hand back and started drawing energy from across a myriad of crossworlds. The stringworm had consumed her legs almost to the waist by the time she flung her arm toward it, the ball of energy having no distance at all to travel before reaching its target.

There was a blinding flash on impact, then the stringworm doubled in size, its mouth now having reached her chest. The strength of the creature's movements were sucking Patsy deeper into its body, causing Jai's grip around her shoulders to slip. He watched on. In the space of a second, Patsy's head and shoulders disappeared, leaving just her right arm exposed. He grabbed hold of it in a two-handed monkey grip. He felt Patsy clasp her hand tight on his wrist, so much so that her fingernails bit into his flesh.

A moment later, his own arms had disappeared up to the shoulders. Although his arms felt cold, there was also a tingling sensation, almost what he would describe as an electric feeling. The next thing Jai knew, the stringworm had drawn in his whole body, with only his left foot remaining to be consumed. In desperation he'd managed to hook it around a tree. As the stringworm sucked harder, Jai felt his foot slip out of its shoe. Then came the sensation of falling.

Patsy and Jai maintained their grip on each other as they watched differing versions of the area around the creek flash before them. Although inside the stringworm's belly, they could see through it to the outside as they experienced a freefall through the Crossworlds and time.

In some worlds and times, the creek was much as Patsy knew it, in others it was dry, or part of a vast ocean, while in others it was filled with fantastical buildings and strange creatures.

The worlds and times flashed by at a rapidly accelerating pace as the stringworm digested its meal, feasting on the energy generated by their transitions through worlds. Once it had its fill, Patsy and Jai were ejected to a world in a time and place that neither recognised.

CHAPTER 3

G ladys Taylor settled into the seat of the sulky and took the reins. She looked down at her husband and smiled. "Are you sure you'd rather not be joining me?" she asked.

Captain Taylor closed his eyes and rubbed his brow. "It's humiliating enough having to call you my wife. I'll be damned if I'm going to let that pathetic scum who should have swung from the gallows bear witness to my torture."

Gladys leaned down and said, "Such a shame you see it that way. I'm learning to find the lighter side of our situation."

The captain looked up. "Well then, do us both a favour and get this over with. Find the worm and get rid of that wretched little witch so I can send you back to Sydney and we can be free of each other."

Gladys flicked the reins and the sulky began moving forward. She looked over her shoulder. A broad grin grew across her face. "Don't worry, I'll find the stringworm. It'll be close to the portal for sure. I don't know that I'll be in such a rush to be wanting to leave my husband's side, though. The soldiers all seem to think we make a grand looking couple." A haunting cackle filled the air as she rode off.

*

Jai ran his hand over the hard ground they had landed on. "It feels cold like cast iron." He looked across at Patsy. "I think it must be some kind of road."

She looked around and asked, "Where are the trees?"

Jai replied, "Forget about the trees, what was that? What just happened?"

"The only thing I know for sure is that we got dragged through too many crossworlds to count. But something else happened, too, something unfamiliar to me."

"What, like getting swallowed by some weird leech-like creature that displaces time?"

"That's it!" Patsy leaped to her feet. "Time! We've been dragged through time, as well."

"So, we've travelled across worlds, and through time, but we're effectively in the same place?" asked Jai.

"I think so."

"The portal, do you think there might be one here as well, in the same place?"

Patsy shrugged. "I don't know."

Jai smiled. "I've got an idea." He pulled his phone from the pocket of his borrowed trousers. "When I was close to the portal in our world and time, I could pick up a signal."

"Pick up a signal? What's that meant to mean? Could you please explain that in a way that makes sense?"

Jai ignored her as he unlocked his phone and stared at it as though willing it to find a signal. "It's there, but it's very weak." He stood up and looked around. "The good news is, that means the portal is here. It must be."

"I can't see any sign of the creek anywhere."

Jai pointed. "Look, over there."

Patsy looked to where he was pointing. There was the rock, the one where Patsy had rescued a fairy two years earlier in her own world. It was surrounded by a mass of green slime. "It looks like there's water in there."

"Ewww!" said Jai. He pinched his nose to block out the smell as they approached the stagnant pool. He looked down at his phone again. "The signal's definitely stronger as we get closer." He tapped on the screen and said, "I'm turning on a tracking app." Seeing the frown on Patsy's face, it was clear to him that she'd need an explanation. "The tracking app will record how far we move and in what direction... without relying on satellites." Patsy's expression hadn't changed. "Look, what matters is that it'll help us get back here if we have to move away for some reason." He slipped his phone back into his pocket and asked, "What was that thing anyway... you know, the thing that sucked us up and transported us here?"

Patsy shook her head. "I don't know. I've never heard of anything like it."

"Whatever it was, it's not featured in any wildlife docos I've ever seen."

His comment was met with another angry glare.

Jai opened his mouth, ready to provide an explanation, but then thought better of it.

An uncomfortable silence followed that felt like it lasted an eternity. Then, Patsy grabbed Jai's shoulder and pointed to a giant slug moving toward them through the thick green fog that obscured their surroundings. "What's that?"

Jai took a small step forward. "I don't know, but it looks a bit like it might have a human on its back." The slug was as big as a small house. It had reins, a bridle, and an elaborate saddle like you would expect of a horse in a parade for a monarch. A rider sat in the saddle wearing red military clothing similar to what the British soldiers wore in the American War of Independence. The face was hidden by a leather gas mask with large goggles.

The rider, holding what appeared to be a stockwhip, pointed at Patsy and Jai then yelled, "Bash wah!"

Jai looked at Patsy. "Any idea what he's saying?"

"She's telling us to stand up."

"She? How do you know?"

"I can sense it." Patsy tightened her grip on Jai's shoulder. "I suggest we do as she's asking."

"Do you recognise the language?"

"No, I just know how to listen. If you listen properly, every language makes sense, even animals."

"My grandmother says that, too. She reckons the birds in her garden always talk to her. Mum and I always thought she was just a bit on the crazy side."

"Vestey!"

Jai asked, "What was—"

The whip unfurled and a moment later was wrapped around Jai and

Patsy. Patsy whispered, "She said 'silence.'"

The rider turned her stead and dragged the tightly bound Patsy and Jai into the fog.

*

Colin, Meredith, Neridah and Clara stood on the front veranda watching Gladys Taylor's sulky approach.

Meredith asked, "Why does it have to be her?"

Colin replied, "We both know why."

Clara looked from one to the other. "I'm still confused as to why you let Patricia go into hiding. What could she possibly have to fear when we're all present?"

Neridah continued watching the sulky as it came to a stop. Darcy made his way across from the stables to help Gladys Taylor down from the seat. Neridah glanced at Clara and replied, "I just hope you don't end up with a full answer to that. You've had enough surprises for one day."

As Clara watched the older woman in the heavy blue dress approach, she shielded her eyes, sure that the midday sun must have been playing tricks on her. There was something about the woman's shadow that disturbed her. She looked across at the other three who stood with her. "Do you see it?" she whispered to Colin, who was standing to her left.

"See what?"

"The shadow." As Clara turned back to face Gladys Taylor, the shadow's arms stretched out toward her in a way she knew was not possible when the sun was almost directly overhead. The jaws of the shadow's head opened wide, revealing a hideous array of sharp silhouetted teeth. She reached for her chest as her knees collapsed under her.

Colin managed to get an arm under Clara's shoulder before she blacked out completely.

Meredith raced into the house calling out, "Cook, we need cold water and wet towels. Miss Jenkins has passed out."

While Neridah and Colin lay Clara down on the veranda, Gladys came up the stairs and asked, "Would I be right in my assumption that this is the tutor?"

Neridah glared back at her. "A bit of concern would be welcome."

Gladys put her arms out as Darcy carried her bags up the stairs. "Welcome? Yes, a welcome would be nice. I accompanied my husband up from Sydney for the express purpose of seeing to it that a girl who appears absent is being properly tutored by a young woman who, it would seem, is incapable of dealing with the midday sun."

Colin looked at the bags. "I would hope you don't have any thoughts that you'll be staying here overnight. There's ample accommodation available in town."

Gladys walked straight past him and entered the house uninvited. "I'd appreciate a brandy while I wait for the girl to appear and for the tutor to recover."

Cook came out to the veranda with a jug of water and a wet towel. "Don't worry yourself, Mr McIntyre, sir. I'll look after her from here and see to her comfort when she comes to."

Colin looked at Neridah and whispered, "I should go inside and see to our guest's comfort. Can you make your way to the creek? Someone needs to check on Patricia and Jai. I've a bad feeling."

Neridah rose to her feet and made her way down the paddock toward the pathway leading to the pool and the creek that fed into it.

Gladys walked into the sitting room and looked toward the window. She smiled at the sight of Neridah walking through the paddock. If the young witch had chosen to hide near the portal and the stringworm had been attracted to it, then maybe things were destined to work out as planned after all.

.

"It smells like mint." Jai stared into the mist, sniffing as their captor hauled them along.

Patsy stumbled, pulling Jai to the ground with her. The slug continued its slow progress forward, dragging them along while they struggled to get back on their feet. "Can we focus on just trying to keep moving rather than what the fog smells or tastes like? It's not like I hadn't noticed." They were forced by the whip that bound them to walk sideways with their backs to each other. The leather of the whip was already making the flesh on Patsy's arm raw.

"Vestey!" The rider glared at them while holding up a blowpipe in a threatening manner.

Once the rider had turned forward again, Jai whispered, "Can't you use some magic or something?"

"Or something?" Patsy whispered back.

"You know, allow yourself to be somewhere or whatever."

"Whatever?" Patsy wanted Jai to see her face, so he could see just how ridiculous she thought his comment was. "You really think it's that simple?"

"I've read your books... you make it seem so simple in them."

"What do you mean, my books?"

"About your life, and how you learned about magic. You've written about a dozen from memory. I've read them all."

"Oh, really?"

"Yeah, the first one was called *Sellemae's Wrath*."

"Why would I want to write a book about that horrid creature?"

"I don't know, you tell me."

Patsy took a deep breath and spoke through clenched teeth. "You have no idea how annoying it is to have you tell me about something I haven't done yet and behave as though I should know all about it."

"Hey, what's your problem?"

"You're my problem!" Patsy's breaths were getting short and sharp.

"VESTEY!" The rider brought the blowpipe to her lips.

Oblivious to the rider and the blowpipe, Patsy stamped her foot. "I've had enough!" The ground shook, sending a shock wave up through the slug that threw the rider off balance as she blew into her pipe. A dart flew past Patsy's ear as she burst free of the stockwhip and pointed at Jai. "Krinkle-myst told you not to tell me about things I'm going to do in the future."

Jai turned to face her and put his hands in front of himself in a defensive gesture. "Hey, calm down will you."

"Calm down? You expect me to calm down?"

Jai pointed to the rider. "I can see you're upset, but can't we deal with this little problem first?"

Without looking, Patsy pushed a hand in the direction of the rider, sending a burst of energy forth that knocked her from her saddle.

"What captor?" Patsy's eyes bore into Jai so deep that he found himself backing away.

"Hey, my plan worked, okay?"

"What plan?" Her breathing was getting heavier. Energy was building around her hands that hung by her side.

"In the books, they said that when you get angry you sometimes release a burst of power."

Patsy responded with more heavy breaths delivered through clenched teeth. She was drawing back her right hand, her eyes still trained on Jai, when a giant hairy caterpillar landed behind him. It took them both by surprise.

Patsy yelled, "Duck!"

She lunged forward, hurling a ball of energy at the creature. No sooner had it been sent hurtling back than another had fallen and landed between them. It reared up, lifting its head high above Patsy, then opened its jaws. Jai had crash tackled it, bringing it to the ground. More caterpillars started falling, surrounding the two teenagers. One had reared up over Jai, but Patsy brought forth her left hand and sent it hurtling back. Again and again caterpillars reared up, only to have Patsy send them back. But Jai wasn't getting up. More caterpillars fell, some up them landing on the slug's back. The animal was screaming in pain as they crawled over its back.

"Flade." The rider was calling out to them and gesturing for them to follow her.

"Jai, we need to go."

He raised his head. "Urrgh…" He struggled to lift himself to an elbow.

"Are you okay?" Looking at his flesh told her he was anything but okay. Everywhere his skin had made contact with the caterpillar was now red and swollen with large lumps. Patsy grabbed hold of his arm, put it across the back of her neck, then grabbed him around the waist and tried to lift. Another caterpillar reared up, ready to lunge at them. A dart from the rider's blowpipe struck it in the eye, causing it to release a high-pitched scream. Jai was dead weight as Patsy started toward the rider. The adrenalin surging through her veins was all that allowed her to move forward. Passing the slug, she saw the caterpillars tearing away at its flesh. The life seemed to drain away from its cries. The rider came to her aide and took Jai's other arm over her shoulder.

The rider said, "Flade, lil sis bo carpee." *Hurry, or else he dies.* With the two of them supporting Jai, they managed to break into a laboured run from the scene. The caterpillars seemed more concerned by the feast they had captured than pursuing them.

•

The Reverend was tightening the strap on Elsa's saddle when a voice called from behind him. "I was hoping we could talk before you go to the McIntyres."

The Reverend turned. "Bordauex? I'll happily delay my departure, if only briefly, to share some words."

"I wish to follow in your path… to become a priest of this church."

The Reverend raised a heavy grey eyebrow in surprise. "So, you believe in what you have read of the Messiah?"

"I have read of many messiahs in many worlds. I believe in the shining light that they give to their followers. Whether the tales are factual or fabrications is not important to me. I care about the spreading of good messages in a way that people may respond to."

The Reverend nodded and looked to the ground for a moment as he collected his thoughts. He then looked Bordauex in the eye. "The thoughts you have expressed are not the thoughts that the Church wants to hear when someone expresses their wish to be ordained as a priest." He placed a hand on his disciple's shoulder. "But your heart is in very much the same place as my own. If being a priest is what you want, then I believe you'll make a fine one. I'll do all that I can to help you."

"Can you then train me?"

The Reverend put his left boot into the stirrup of Elsa's saddle, then mounted the horse. "No, that is something I cannot do. There is a seminary in Sydney where you can be trained. That is the only way. I'll make sure to contact the bishop and see what I can do to help you get a place there." Before Bordauex had a chance to respond, the Reverend had kicked his heels into Elsa's side and headed off toward the McIntyre property.

.

"What were those creatures?" asked Patsy in the rider's language.

"Oh, so you can speak the true words?"

"I need to only listen for a while before I can speak a language."

"There is only one language, everything else is akin to the noises animals make to each other."

Patsy opened her mouth to respond in a reflex reaction to the rider's closed-minded attitude. She managed to stop herself before the first words spilled out. *I need this woman's help if Jai's to have any chance of survival.* "Those creatures, what were they?"

The rider stopped and stared at Patsy through her grimy gasmask. Her voice muffled by its multi-layered filters that gave it an electronic sound. "How could the Enchantress not know of wrathapillars?"

"Enchantress?"

"Unlike most of our rebellious youth, I have bothered to study the prophecies of the ancients. 'She will be unknown until she breaks her bonds and strikes down her enemies with the power that comes from her hands.' Is that not what you have just done?"

"I very much doubt that my arrival here is what was foretold."

"We'll see what the Seer has to say when we reach the citadel."

Again, Patsy refrained from saying what first came to mind. She tried to bring the conversation back to the urgency of Jai's needs. "Is there a doctor at the citadel?"

"You use the words in a strange way. Your beast of burden needs a healer, not a doctor."

"He's no beast of burden. He's my friend."

The rider looked at Jai and sneered. "I've yet to meet a male who is not a burden."

"Well, then I'm sad for you. The reason he's hurt is because he put himself in harm's way to protect me. You were there. You saw him tackle the 'wrathapillar,' as you call it."

"And that is the only reason I'm prepared to risk my own status by taking him to the healer."

"We have just arrived here from far away. Where I come from, males and females are more equal."

The rider looked Patsy up and down. "You don't look like a coast dweller. But your clothes and use of words are strange. I know of no culture where a woman would call a male a friend." After a long pause she asked, "Where do you come from?"

"I come from this same place, but on a different plane and from a different time."

"I don't doubt that there is likely a truth in what you say, for you clearly are the Enchantress. But I won't pretend to understand. That is the job of the Seer, and hopefully she will help me to comprehend."

They walked on in silence, carrying the now unconscious Jai, whose feet dragged along the ground as they moved forward.

The green fog began to thin out, revealing a forest of what appeared to be gigantic mint plants. Up ahead, a massive wall loomed that appeared to be made of the same material as the ground they'd been walking on. An ornate gate dominated the wall ahead of them. "Why the wall?" asked Patsy.

"I don't understand the question."

"The wall, why do you need it?"

"What meaning would life have without it?"

Patsy wished she hadn't asked.

"Halt, and state your business in the city."

"I am Keesnah, returning from patrol."

"Where be your stead?"

"Taken by wrathapillars."

"Who else accompanies you to the city gate?"

"I bring with me the Enchantress, whose coming was foretold. Her beast of burden is injured."

The gate opened a small amount and a round mechanical contraption approached the trio. It was covered in knobs and dials, with large keys for winding springs located in several spots around its spherical base. It moved as if on wheels, although Patsy couldn't locate where the wheels might be. A light rose out of the top and Patsy was blinded for a few seconds when it flashed. The contraption then retreated back through the gate which closed behind it.

"What now?" asked Patsy.

"We wait for approval. I have lost my steed. We will not be admitted into the city unless the Seer wishes to interview you."

.

Gladys downed her brandy in an unladylike fashion. She held the glass out toward Colin and asked, "Could I trouble you for another while we wait for the tutor and your daughter?"

Colin grimaced as he remembered the last time they had an unwelcomed guest who enjoyed downing his brandy in such a fashion.

Regardless, he took the glass. "Yes, of course."

Gladys walked across to the window as Colin made his way to the small table where the brandy decanter sat. She smiled as she watched Neridah run up the paddock, waving her arms in a state of panic. Meredith met her halfway. Colin approached the window, handing Gladys her drink on the way. He glanced out at the scene unfolding in the paddock, then said, "Please excuse me, it seems there are things I must attend to."

Gladys threw down the second drink in the same way she had done with the first. "So it would seem. And that being the case, I think I shall leave and return another day when your tutor is better prepared."

"I'll only be a few minutes—"

"No, I'll be on my way." She strode past Colin and made her way out of the house, picking up her bags from where Darcy had left them just inside the front door. She ignored Cook and Clara as she carried her bags down the stairs, then tossed them onto the sulky in a haphazard fashion before climbing into the seat and driving off in a hurry.

.

The creaking of the gigantic gate startled Patsy. "What's happening?"

Keesnah turned to Patsy. "Enchantress?"

"Oh, sorry. I'd drifted off into a daydream. I wasn't quite sure where I was for a moment."

"It is written that the Enchantress inhabits many worlds. Perhaps your mind had drifted to another."

A dozen soldiers marched out, two carrying a canvas stretcher. They placed it on the ground next to Jai, then lifted him up and laid him on it. Another two clapped irons on Keesnah's ankles then placed a hessian sack over her head before marching her into the darkness within the gate. A woman who appeared to be a captain of some sort addressed Patsy. "The Seer will see you now."

Patsy looked at Jai. "And what about my friend?"

"The healer will see to his survival if the Seer is satisfied."

"Satisfied?"

"That you are indeed the Enchantress."

Patsy looked at Keesnah disappearing into the shadows with the soldiers. "And her?"

"Her fate will be decided by those who study the scriptures. That is to say, if the Seer deems you true."

"What if she doesn't?"

"Then she will be declared a burden."

Patsy needed to meet the Seer as soon as possible if there was to be any hope of Jai getting treatment. She looked down at her descendant. *I'm so sorry this has happened to you.*

The point of a spear against Patsy's back told her it was time to start walking. As she passed through the massive cast iron gates, her eyes adjusted to the dim light. There were hundreds of people gathered in silence to watch her entrance. Up ahead she saw what appeared to be a grand cathedral. Like the gate and the roads, it was made of cast iron.

"She has come to save us!" called a voice from the crowd. Everyone turned and pointed to the culprit. She cringed as the crowd parted to make way for an approaching soldier. "Please, I wish only to honour that which has been foretold."

"You blaspheme against your monarch." The soldier punched the woman in the stomach, causing her to double over in pain, then addressed the crowd. "See to it that she wears her shame till the moon has twice been full."

The crowd continued pointing at her and began chanting, "Shame, shame, shame..."

"ENOUGH!" The crowd went silent and turned to face the cathedral. An old woman dressed in orange robes with gold embroidered trim was descending the stairs. She carried a large staff topped with an orange crystal. Despite her age, her voice boomed with authority. "Let no woman cast judgement on another this day until we know whether the Enchantress is truly among us."

An instant later, Patsy and her escort had been transported to the steps of the cathedral, just below where the old Seer stood with her staff. "You know magic!" gasped Patsy.

The Seer smiled at Patsy. "You speak as one who understands such things. Come, allow yourself to join me inside, away from the brutality of these thugs."

A moment later, Patsy and the Seer were seated in a gallery that overlooked the altar of the church. A ceremonial fire burned behind them in an ornate cast iron bowl that sat atop a pillar twice Patsy's height. "My friend, can you save him?"

The Seer shook her head. "No, he is not of this world. The only one who can save him is you."

"But I don't know how."

"Perhaps with some guidance you might. He can only be saved by one who knows him walking inside his mind and waking his soul."

"Can you help me to do that?"

"I can help you and he prepare. But the real help you need comes from a book." The Seer gestured to a golden shroud that covered a bookstand. "If the book accepts you, you will find the wisdom you need."

Patsy rose to her feet then approached the bookstand. She took a deep breath before raising the shroud. "No! It can't be!" She dropped the shroud then turned back to the Seer. "It's the Book of Wisdom! How can it be here?"

The Seer laughed. "Didn't the wood-elf tell you the truth of the book? It exists in many worlds, and thus contains many points of view. How could it contain true wisdom if its words came just from one world's understanding?"

"So, this is the same as the one I'm familiar with?"

"Seeing I have read many of your passages, Patricia, or should I say, Patsy McIntyre, one would assume so."

"And, you know Krinkle-myst?"

"Is that what he calls himself?" Again, the Seer smiled. "All I know is, a wood-elf came to me in a dream and warned me of your coming."

"Warned you? That doesn't sound good."

"No, it doesn't, does it?"

•

Neridah arrived at the stables at the same time as the Reverend. "Patricia's gone!"

The Reverend could see the panic in Neridah's eyes as he dismounted Elsa. "What are you talking about? How is she gone?"

"Patricia and Jai. They went for a walk to hide from Mrs Taylor, who it turns out used to be Mrs Bradshaw, the tutor that Patricia couldn't get on with. Remember? She's the one who had been possessed by a mind thief. After Mrs Taylor left, we went looking for them. We can't find them anywhere, just some footprints down by the creek where they went to hide."

The Reverend nodded thoughtfully and leaned forward in the saddle. As he considered the news, he looked up and asked, "Have you made enquiries with the fairies?"

Neridah sneered and looked away. "That would mean talking to Mrs Smith. Can't Bandah and the pixies help instead?"

The Reverend handed Elsa's reins to Darcy who'd just emerged from the darkness of the stables. "It seems Bandah is somewhat distracted by other issues of late." He rubbed at his bearded chin. "With regards to Mrs Smith, is it not worthwhile dealing with the likes of her if it might help us find your granddaughter?"

"She's your gran—"

Neridah was interrupted by a voice with less volume, as though from someone much smaller. "You always talk about me as though I'm not here." The Reverend and Neridah looked down to see the old fairy that was Mrs Smith standing, hands on hips, just a few paces away from them.

Neridah glared at the fairy. Her fists clenched as all her muscles tightened. "Perhaps you would find that happened less often if you made your presence known before listening in to others' conversations."

"Hmmph!" Mrs Smith adopted a similar pose to the one Neridah had struck. "Perhaps I'd be more upfront about my presence if your words were generally kinder."

The Reverend closed his eyes and nodded in agreement. "Aye, I must admit, it would seem there is some truth in that."

Neridah's jaw dropped. "You must be joking!"

The only response she got was a raised and heavy grey eyebrow.

"I spent forty years bound up in a cocoon because of her. She kept us apart for four decades. I tried to help her, and she betrayed me. Haven't we both suffered enough as a result of her deceit?"

Mrs Smith shook her head. "I nearly died trying to help you deal with Kerridwen. Oh, and your pixie friend, Bandah? He would still be stuck in the void were it not for me."

Neridah rolled her eyes. "Oh, what a saint you are! I can't believe you would even consider comparing that to what Alfred and I went through thanks to your betrayal."

Mrs Smith said, "That's not what this is about. The girl's gone missing. I don't know where she is, but I want to help, and I think I might have a clue."

"I don't need to hear more of your lies." Neridah looked away.

The Reverend shook his head. "Can you not hear yourself, woman? I think you're being unnecessarily unkind."

"If that's how you feel, then I'm finished with this conversation." Neridah turned and stormed off toward the house.

The Reverend looked up to the sky as though it may deliver an answer to the question he didn't want to ask.

"So, do you want to know?" The fairy stood with her arms folded, her voice carrying the smug tone that suggested she knew she was now in control of the situation.

The Reverend turned his gaze toward Mrs Smith, then took a deep breath and closed his eyes. He reminded himself that anger would not help him convince the fairy to tell him what she knew. He opened his eyes and squatted to bring himself closer to her level. "Aye, I would very much like to know."

"I didn't see it myself, but I heard a rumour. My sisters were concerned. They see people coming from another time as a poor omen, so weren't prepared to keep a watch on the two of them themselves." She paused, as though wanting to wait for clarification that the Reverend understood.

"Go on, I'm listening."

"So, they asked a magpie to keep watch and report back to them." An uneasy pause followed before Mrs Smith took a deep breath and continued. "The magpie said it watched a worm, or a leech of some kind. It watched the creature devour them whole, but without increasing in size once they were consumed. It said that it was as though they were transported to another world."

The Reverend slowly rose to his feet. He'd never heard of such a thing before. "As hard as it is to believe what you're saying, I see no reason why you'd seek to deceive me right now."

"Thank you." Mrs Smith reached out and grabbed his trouser leg. "Despite everything from the past, I truly do wish to be of help."

The Reverend nodded in acknowledgement as he started to meander toward the house, pondering how to break the news to Patsy's family.

*

Silence hung over the crowd for several seconds after the Seer and Patsy disappeared. A lone voice then called out, "It's true, she really is the Enchantress that was foretold."

The crowd as one turned toward the woman who had spoken out. A pair of soldiers marched up to her and dragged her to the top of the stairs.

One of the soldiers addressed the crowd. "Do you before us declare that you have witnessed this one blaspheme?"

The crowd chanted, "Guilty as charged. Guilty as charged. Guilty…"

As the crowd continued their chant, a young woman, barely past the age of independent thought, strode through the middle of the crowd and up the stairs. She then turned to face them and called out, "All she is guilty of is speaking the truth." Shocked by the boldness of one so young, the crowd fell back to silence. "We have all seen for ourselves, the Enchantress is real. She disappeared and took the Seer with her." The crowd began murmuring among themselves. "The Seer has not dared to display her power in nearly fifty rotations around the sun. Surely this is a sign that we should stand up to those who have enslaved us for so—" She fell to the ground with a dart in the side of her neck.

A bugle sounded from the top of a building adjacent to the cathedral. It was less than half the church's height, but still imposing. A soldier wearing the trappings of high status within the military walked onto the building's upper balcony and held up a gigantic megaphone. A hollow electronic projection of her voice rang out over the square. "The population within this area is guilty of allowing one of its own to speak a heresy. Two score will now pay the price."

A battalion of soldiers rushed out of the building and collected forty women at random and dragged them into the shadows. The scene played out in eerie silence; no one wished to draw attention to themselves.

.

Gladys rode the sulky over the small bridge that crossed the creek a few minutes down the road from the McIntyre property. She led the horse and sulky down a side-track which travellers sometimes used to lead the horses to the creek for water. Once sure that the sulky was out of sight, she grabbed a glass jar from her bag and began making her way down the creek in search of the stringworm. She felt confident that if it had just enjoyed a meal, it would be more content to remain in the jar once captured.

It was slow going walking through the creek with the heavy dress weighing her down as it absorbed ever more water. She would have removed it were it not so difficult to do so. It was at times like this that the Nasqa holding her mind captive most missed its days as a gravedigger with all the simplicity that life had offered. She was halfway back to the McIntyre property when she heard voices approaching. *Damn that man's tenacity*, she thought. It sounded like Colin had enlisted the help of the stablehands in his bid to find his daughter. Gladys crouched low and pushed herself into the gap between the buttressed roots of a large tree. She closed her eyes and imagined the anger she'd have to face from her husband once she'd been caught and returned to him without the stringworm. A cold and empty feeling on the tip of her ring finger drew her attention.

No, it couldn't be!

The stringworm had already made her whole finger disappear as she struggled to get the lid off the jar. She hoped she might still be able to get it off her finger and capture it.

Then, the jar was gone, as was the hand holding it. Both arms were now consumed up to the elbows.

The voices were getting closer.

She had no choice. She'd have to either call out for help or accept being thrown into another time and plane with no hope of return. As she opened her mouth to call out, the world disappeared, and she found herself falling through an abyss. Countless worlds flashed by. It felt like an eternity had passed when she hit the ground with a thud. She coughed as she tried to breathe the methane-laden atmosphere. And the heat—it was sweltering, unbearably hot with clouds of fire filling the sky.

CHAPTER 4

Patsy closed her eyes and strained with the effort as she dragged the Book of Wisdom open to the page she had selected in her mind. She ran a finger over the soft vellum, feeling as though she could read the ink lettering with her fingertips. The young witch opened her eyes and scanned the page. "This can't be."

"Is it not as I told you it would be?" asked the Seer.

Patsy nodded. "It says that I have to allow myself to go inside his mind and become one with him." She turned and faced the Seer. "Are you sure this is the only way?"

The Seer took a deep breath and placed a withered hand on Patsy's shoulder. "He has reacted badly to the wrathapiller's poison. Far worse than any I have saved before. He is beyond the lotions I would normally apply being of any use."

"But you haven't even tried." The shakiness in Patsy's voice betrayed her desperation.

"Look at him, Patricia McIntyre, Crossworld Witch, Enchantress that the scriptures foretold, and then try to tell me that I lie."

Patsy wept as she looked at the unconscious boy who lay on a cot in the corner of the gallery. She walked the few paces it took to be by his side, then held his hand. It was cold, with little sign of life. She could see that the Seer was right. "What if I fail?"

"That's the wrong question."

Knowing the Seer was right, Patsy knelt down and closed her eyes and whispered, "You have to make it through this." Her words were for both Jai and herself. She took a breath, then allowed herself to be one with her descendent.

.

The Reverend and Neridah stood looking over Meredith's shoulder. She closed her eyes and ran her hand down the edge of the pages in the ornate and ancient Book of Wisdom, feeling for which one she should turn to. Using both hands, she opened the book to the page she'd sought in her mind.

At the top of the right-hand page was an illustration of a leech-like creature devouring a human forearm. The three of them gasped together as they stared at the illustration. They had to wait while they absorbed the page before them enough to read the language they'd never seen before. It was written in a script that had little in common with any they'd previously encountered in the book.

Neridah was the first to be able to translate the ancient script. "It's called a stringworm."

The three of them were all now able to read the text, digesting its words and trying to make sense of the strange syntax as they went.

Meredith held a hand against her heart as she said, "I feel more confident they're alive now."

The Reverend asked, "Aye, but where are they?"

Neridah replied, "According to this, they could be anywhere. It talks about not just different crossworlds, but different times and timelines."

The Reverend said, "It tells us nothing of how to find them."

Neridah said, "We need to search elsewhere in the book."

Meredith nodded in agreement, then closed her eyes as she again ran her fingers down the edge of the book while thinking about finding someone lost in place and time. She opened the book to another page, one that was dense with small text and the occasional equation that appeared similar to what one might find in a physics textbook.

"This will take time to make sense of," said the Reverend.

"We don't have time," replied Neridah.

Meredith turned to her mother. "We don't know that. We don't even know for sure that they were consumed by that thing."

Neridah's eyes narrowed as she prepared to counter her daughter. Then she felt the Reverend's firm hand on her shoulder. "Let's not bicker. To know one way or the other, we'll need to decipher this text."

Neridah bit her lower lip as she nodded in agreement.

Meredith said, "I'm going to grab a journal and take notes."

The Reverend agreed. "Aye, that's a good idea. I might do the same."

The three of them spent the next three hours reading, writing notes, and discussing points that made little sense on first reading. They were debating one particular point when there was a knock at the door. "I'll get it," said Meredith.

As Meredith made her way to the door, Neridah said to the Reverend,

"It's not worth the risk. We could end up lost in the void forever."

The Reverend replied, "I understand your reasons for feeling that way, and that's why I say we should take the book with us, just in case."

Meredith opened the door to see Colin's concerned face. "How's Clara?" asked Meredith.

"I think she's fine now. She said she saw Mrs Taylor's shadow move like it was the shadow of a monster. You know what that means," said Colin with a note of concern in his voice.

At the far end of the library, Neridah pointed to Meredith and lowered her voice to a whisper. "How can we be sure that you replacing Patricia in the Trilogy will even work?"

"It will work as long as she's replaced by someone of the same bloodline." The voice came from a small wood-elf who'd appeared at their feet. The Reverend and Neridah looked down at him, disbelief etched into their expressions. "I don't normally make house calls, but those two kids have created a hell of a mess. And I'd really like to see it cleaned up before it's too late to save this world and countless others."

Unaware of Krinkle-myst's appearance, Meredith slipped outside the library and pulled the door shut behind her. "Yes, and I must say, it comes as little surprise. It also confirms all our worst fears about the governor."

Colin asked her, "Have you had any luck?"

Back inside the room, debate was continuing. The Reverend looked at Krinkle-myst and said, "So, judging by what you say, it will indeed work if I take Patricia's place in the Trilogy."

The wood-elf shrugged his shoulders. "It's the only way you'll have a chance of tuning in to her among the vastness of all places and times."

"We've kept this truth secret for all these years." Neridah looked to the door, thinking of her daughter on the other side.

The Reverend replied, "She has to learn of the truth sometime."

"But does it have to be today? And what if we're wrong?"

Krinkle-myst reassured her. "I can tell you now, your granddaughter and Jai will sooner or later look to form a Trilogy themselves, wherever they are. While the time and world they've gone to can't be predicted, the geographic location can be. It will align to where we are now. And they more than likely will come across someone of the same bloodline and form their own Trilogy."

"How can you be sure of this?" asked the Reverend.

"Because it's already written as the most likely future history."

Neridah sighed then looked at the Reverend. "Well, it looks like it's time we have a little discussion with my daughter about the truth."

Outside, Meredith looked to the floor as she considered what to say. She then made direct eye contact as she told Colin what she knew of Patsy's fate in as few words as she could. "Patricia and Jai are lost in place and time. The only way we can find them is if Alfred, Mother and myself form our own Trilogy and surrender ourselves to the void. It's the only way that she'll ever be able to tune into the right time and place to return as we'd still be anchored to this one. We'd be like a beacon."

"Then why does it appear there's still debate going on?"

"If we're unsuccessful in finding her, there's a risk that we'll be unable to get back from the void. Being within the void requires someone outside of it to pull you out."

"I see." Colin nodded, then rubbed at his chin before asking, "What do you think?"

"I don't think there's any other choice."

"Then you have my support. Go, go and find our daughter."

*

"Jai?" Patsy looked around her and saw nothing but emptiness; her voice echoing through the void suggested that the empty space had boundaries. She took a few small and tentative steps forward. "Are you in here?"

A little girl's voice behind her said, "He's here. You just need to wake him." Patsy turned to see a girl with long dark hair wearing a white dress who wouldn't be older than four or five.

"Who are you?"

"I'm the Seer. I came to help you find him."

"But you're so young."

"My body can't survive if I leave it fully, so I could only send a small part of me."

"Well, thank you."

"There's another reason I came to join you."

"What's that?"

"We can talk in here without anyone hearing us."

"We were on our own in the cathedral's gallery too."

"No, we weren't," said the girl, "the soldiers have listening devices everywhere. They won't tolerate dissent."

"But aren't you revered by them?"

"They tolerate me, barely. They see my magic as a threat to their power, and accept my presence only if I toe the line and support their agenda."

"Can't you stop them?"

"I am old and on my own. I don't have enough strength. They killed my offspring when they were born because the scriptures foretold a Trilogy of Power that would oust them."

"Is that the same scripture that the rider I came across outside said foretold my coming?"

"Yes." She looked up at Patsy with sorrowful eyes. "Few understand its true meaning. They interpret the Trilogy as meaning I have offspring, but the truth is different. The Trilogy is formed after the arrival of the Enchantress. That's why it's so important that you save Jai."

"But a Trilogy requires three women of the same bloodline."

"The Book of Wisdom says it needs three generations of the same bloodline. It says nothing about gender."

"Even if that be the case, you and I are from different worlds."

"Different worlds perhaps, but I believe our bloodline is the same. I have traced back my family history and yours through the Book of Wisdom. It is identical until the time the gene cutters changed my world's history a century and a half ago."

"What's a gene cutter?"

"Do they not exist in your world?"

"Not that I know of."

"Do you know much about biology?"

"No, I've always found it quite boring."

"Hmph! Some help you'll be." The little girl who was the Seer grabbed Patsy's hand. "Come, we need to find Jai within this darkness before the soldiers realise what we're doing."

"With him not responding to my calls, I've no idea where to look. It's so dark in here."

"You need to find his energy veins."

"His what?"

"The focal points of his energy. Do you not know of them? Have your mother and grandmother taught you nothing?" The Seer reached out a finger and ran it along an imaginary line that ran from below Patsy's waist to above her head. As the girl's hand moved up, eight times Patsy felt a surge of energy between the girl's finger and a point within her that correlated with the path of the Seer's gesture. Each surge of energy felt unique and of varying strength, with the strongest surge coming from above her head. "It is through these energy veins that all living things draw the power that gives them life, and as the Enchantress, you can channel far more than others. Have you never wondered about how the energy you draw from the Crossworlds is channelled through your being? You must find these points within Jai and feed him from your own energy that he may again find his own."

"Why do I feel them now, when I'm already outside of my body?"

"The vision of yourself maintains a connection. Your body feels what your projection feels, and your projection feels what your body feels."

Patsy looked around her. "I guess that makes sense... in a strange kind of way. But how will I find them within Jai? Where do I look?"

"Don't look, feel. Feel each of your own energy veins and you will be drawn to his. That's if you allow it to be so."

Patsy nodded. "Okay, I'll give it a try." She closed her eyes and remembered where the first surge of energy had come from... near the base of her spine. She focused on the sensation and, despite the fact that her consciousness was already projected within Jai, she descended within herself on another layer. She focused on that one particular energy source and omitted all else from her mind. A moment later she became aware of the energy surrounding her, albeit very weak. She could sense the energy was in fact Jai's... that she had transported herself to his lowest energy vein. She opened her eyes and saw a disc of pulsing energy swirling around her. It reminded her of pictures in a book Miss Jenkins had shown her of the rings around Saturn. Only this ring was dim, as though ready to fade out altogether. Patsy focused again on her corresponding energy vein and then thought of her wish to share it with

Jai. She could feel it emanating from the base of her spine and merging with Jai's, causing it to glow and spread.

"Good, you can move to the next one." The Seer's voice sounded distant, yet remained clear.

Without a word, Patsy focused on the next energy vein and repeated the procedure… again and again until she reached the vein behind the eyes.

"Be careful with this one, it will likely cause him to stir, and he may react with fear if he senses our presence."

"Then I'll reach out to him in an effort to soothe his fears." As Patsy repeated the procedure, she noticed something altogether different. A pulse of energy rose up through each of the energy veins, connecting them and flooding the darkness with colourful light in hues that defied description. Patsy couldn't help herself, she reached out with open palms, allowing the soothing energy to flow over them.

"Quickly! You must move to the last vein before the energy flow recedes like the tide."

The urgency in the Seer's voice jolted Patsy's mind back to her task. She focused on the crowning vein and found herself shooting upward as though being tossed up by a geyser of light and happiness.

She fell to the floor and realised her consciousness was back within her own body and that she'd been physically thrown back.

Jai was sitting bolt upright, his eyes wide open. "What was that?" he asked between frantic breaths.

The Seer, back within her decrepit frame, replied, "Your ancestor just rescued you from the jaws of certain death."

The main doors to the cathedral swung open with a bang. "Up there, in the gallery… seize them!" More doors were flung open and hundreds of boots thundered into the building. Several of the soldiers took out blowpipes and began firing darts up at the gallery, most of them falling short.

The Seer looked at Patsy and Jai. "We must now be the Trilogy. Both of you, take my hands and we will leave here."

Jai looked to Patsy and, when she nodded her approval, he stood up and took the Seer's hand.

*

"It would have been nice if you'd thought to tell me this sooner." Meredith's eyes were burning with rage.

Neridah reached out to put a hand on her shoulder, only to have it pushed away. "How could I tell you? I was taken away from you for forty years when you were just a baby."

"But you've been back for over two years now." She turned to the Reverend. "And as for you, you have no such excuse. All these years you've lived a lie as the rigid man of the cloth and family friend." She looked him up and down and sneered. "How can you live with yourself?"

The Reverend's voice was an uncharacteristic whisper. "Do you think it's been easy?"

"Try it from where I sit." She collapsed into a chair and burst into tears.

Neridah crouched down next to her daughter. "But we still have to find Patricia. And at least we now know that Alfred's bloodline matches hers."

"We? We now know? It seems to me I'm the only one that's been kept in the dark." She looked at the Reverend. "And don't you think that girl we're looking for deserves to know who you really are? The girl who used to fear you so much? How could you do it... those times you put the fear of God into her when she was younger."

The Reverend remained silent.

Meredith glared at him. "Is that really all you have to say?"

He glanced up. "I think it would be better for all concerned if she remains in the dark in this regard for the time being."

Meredith sneered as she replied, "Better for who?"

Again, the Reverend remained silent. Neridah took his hand in hers. He turned to her. When Neridah saw the forlorn look in his eyes, she leaned in to give him a hug of reassurance, retreating when she sensed his resistance.

Meredith watched on, struggling with how best to deal with this revelation of who her real father was.

This was too big to deal with now.

It would have to wait until she knew her daughter was safe.

She took a few deep breaths then stood up and said, "Okay, let's do this."

·

Destellie's hands lay on Felibrey's shoulders. "You've worked so hard today. It's little wonder you're tired."

Felibrey's yawn was involuntary and long. His eyelids almost obscured his pupils as he replied, "Yes, but it's worthwhile. I do so want to have the cottage finished before our wedding day."

The light of the full moon made the canvas of Felibrey's tent seem to glow behind Destellie's thick mop of dark curls. The lamplight highlighted the softness of her cheeks. "I do too, but are you sure you're not pushing yourself too hard?"

Felibrey put his hands on Destellie's hips and pulled her closer. He found the strength to lift his head and peer into Destellie's eyes, as though reaching in to touch her soul. The sound of frogs and flying foxes celebrating what was an unseasonably warm evening filled the silence while Felibrey searched for his words. "I have never before felt so motivated or driven. It gives me an energy I never knew I could possess."

"My beautiful Felibrey. How could any woman help but love you?" Her eyes closed as their lips came together. Her head swirled as she lost herself for a while in the pleasure of their kiss before her chin finally came to rest on Felibrey's shoulder. They enjoyed the stillness of the moment and the sounds of the night, their hearts beating in perfect rhythm. She gave him a gentle kiss on his neck, then said, "You need to sleep."

Felibrey nodded. "Yes, you're right." They loosened their embrace. "I'll walk you back to your tent."

Destellie took a step back and said, "No, really, I'm fine. You just get yourself to bed. It's only a short walk to my tent."

Again, Felibrey yawned. His eyes were almost shut when he said, "It's really no trouble."

Destellie took his hand and led him the one step it took to reach his cot then placed her hands on his shoulders, pushing him down till he was seated. He lifted his legs and stretched them out, pulling the blanket over himself. He lowered his head to the pillow and said, "As usual, you are right, my love."

Destellie kissed him on the forehead. "Sleep well, beautiful man."

Felibrey's eyes were already closed as he replied, "You too…" Within seconds, his breathing was replaced by a gentle snore.

Destellie waited a few minutes before leaving so as to make sure she didn't wake her fiancé. She emerged from the tent's entrance and looked toward the light at the Reverend's rebuilt house. The light in the windows and the distant sound of revelry told her the other disciples were still enjoying their evening meal and would be there for some time. The moon had only risen a short time ago, so it should be out just long enough for her to make her journey and get back with plenty of time to get an hour or so to sleep before the morning.

*

Instead of the usual instant transportation to where they were allowing themselves to be, the Trilogy of Patsy, Jai, and the Seer found itself caught up in the void between times and places. They were not alone. Jai was staring at the Reverend Alfred Casey, Patsy at her mother, and the Seer at Neridah.

The Reverend peered into Jai's face, studying as one would when seeing something unexpected in the mirror. He turned to Neridah. "You were right. To look at him is akin to looking at a younger version of myself."

Jai said, "I know the truth."

"And you'll not speak of it!" The Reverend's eyes burned with intensity to underscore the importance of his statement.

Patsy looked across and asked, "What truth?"

Meredith said, "The only truth that matters now is that we've found you."

"How?"

Neridah answered for her daughter. "It was Krinkle-myst. He told us that the bloodlines would match well enough for us to connect with you if your mother, Alfred, and I formed our own Trilogy and allowed ourselves to search for a matching one that contained you and Jai." Neridah glanced at the Seer. "You are obviously of our line in your world and time."

The Seer nodded. "The wood-elf gave me similar advice. He said that escape would only be possible if I formed a trilogy with the boy and the Enchantress, and that ours would be strengthened by yours. It made no sense to me at the time, as is always the way when wood-elves are involved."

Meredith said, "Patricia, you need to come home. Then we can send Jai back to his. Once he's gone, you'll need go to an earlier point in that timeline so you can stop him from coming in the first place and prevent the leakage from his reality into our own."

Jai replied. "But the Nasqa are close to taking total control in my world. They have to be stopped. If they unlock the full potential of the Book of Wisdom, they'll be able to follow my path into other timelines. They'll be stronger and harder to stop."

Neridah was firm in her response. "We can show you ways to fight the Nasqa." She turned her attention to Patsy. "We will act as a beacon for you to find your way home. When you're back, we'll need your help to pull us out from the void. Then you can each go where you need to in Jai's timeline and do what must be done."

Patsy asked, "What do you mean?"

Meredith's voice was starting to fade and Patsy struggled to hear what she was saying. "We have to go for now, or we won't be able to find our way back to be near the portal for you. Remember, you'll need Jai's metal box…" Meredith was starting to fade away. Patsy could still see her lips moving but could no longer hear her words.

As the Trilogy of Neridah, Meredith, and the Reverend dissolved into the distance, Jai thought he heard the Reverend's voice in his head. *Keep her safe.*

The darkness lifted, revealing that the Seer, Patsy, and Jai were in a humble wooden cabin with a small fire burning at one end of the room.

The furniture in the cabin was frugal and sparse. Patsy could smell spicy aromas coming from a large pot suspended over the fire on a tripod. Ignoring the hunger that gnawed at her belly, she turned to Jai. "Your phone… do you have it?"

Jai checked his pockets. "It's gone."

The Seer asked, "Are you looking for the magical metal box the boy had in his pocket?"

Patsy retorted, "It's not magic, it's science."

The Seer laughed. "As is all magic when fully understood." She looked toward Jai. "They will have taken your magical box to the Grand Field Commander of the military. She will have her best engineers try to unravel its mysteries as she watches over them." She scratched at her forehead then asked Patsy, "Why is this device so important?"

Jai answered on Patsy's behalf. "Because with it, we can locate the portal and tune it into my crossworld and time. It's the only way we can be sure of getting there."

Patsy tugged at the Seer's sleeve. "We need to go to this Commander and get Jai's phone. We need to do it now."

The Seer nodded her disapproval. "No, they'll be expecting us to try something direct like that. We need to create a distraction."

"Like what?"

The Seer looked up and smiled. "We need to set the beasts of burden free."

*

Twice Destellie had fallen into the creek, the second time grazing her elbow. She had to ensure she got back and took her washing to where the creek ran near the Reverend's property. That was the only way she'd be able to remove the muddy proof of her journey before Felibrey saw her. She'd explain away her injury by saying she'd lost her footing while carrying the basket of clothes. Although she would be tired herself after her long night, the herbs Destellie had slipped into Felibrey's dinner made her confident he would sleep late into the morning.

Now, after a walk of almost three hours, she had reached the pool at the bottom of the McIntyre property.

She sat on a rock to catch her breath and noticed that the frogs and flying foxes had fallen silent. It was only after having stopped that she became conscious of how cold her legs were with the wetness of her dress clinging to them. Her teeth chattered as she wrapped her arms around her shivering shoulders. Glancing up, she saw the moon had passed its zenith. She would have to act now. Destellie stood up and approached the pool's edge, reached down, and grabbed a pebble. Was she doing the right thing? She closed her eyes and thought of Felibrey and her deception. A tear ran down her cheek reminding her of how the emotions that had started as a rouse had now become quite real.

She loved him.

But there was no turning back.

Seeing the pitiful way that the other disciples had embraced this world and been enslaved by its customs filled her with disdain. Bordaeux even wanted to become a Christian priest!

She threw the pebble into the middle of the pool and watched its ripples spread out.

Instead of dissipating, the ripples grew in intensity. The still night became filled with a swirling gale, centred on the pool. Then a massive spray of water surged upward. The spiralling wind captured the water droplets and pushed them around until a shape emerged that hovered larger than life above Destellie. At first, it seemed nondescript. But as the howling wind grew stronger, the features became clear. A haggard vision of Kerridwen, with a garland of angry, snapping daisies, loomed tall. "You're late!"

Destellie went down on her knees and brought her hands together. "Oh, great Queen of the Crossworlds, I have done as you asked, but it took time to win Felibrey's heart, and he is the one who is closest to the priest."

One of the watery daisies in the apparition broke free and flew toward Destellie, turning to flame as it came near. Destellie was forced to push herself flat against the sandy bank at the pool's edge to avoid the flame. Kerridwen's voice carried her fury. "I don't want excuses, just facts. If you want to revel in the power of your own garland, you must do exactly as I say."

Tears were streaming down Destellie's cheeks. "I promise… whatever you wish." She looked up and tried to face the apparition, but the hateful rage that she saw within it compelled her to avert her eyes. Despite her words, she found herself wanting to ensure that, however this played out, she somehow protected Felibrey from the consequences.

"The fools think that the stable-boy, Darcy, is free of my command, but his will remains mine to control. You must use him to help you lure the witches to this spot when next the moon is full, that I may capture them in my garland and thus gain the strength needed to usurp my father." Kerridwen's tone softened. "Then, you will have your garland once more, and the eternal life that goes with it."

The wind died and the water dropped back to the pool. Destellie wept as the sounds of the night returned.

She'd made a big mistake.

She wasn't up to this. As much as she longed for the power of the garland, she now questioned the price.

A gentle hand touched her shoulder. She turned around and saw Darcy. His warm smile reassured her.

"It's okay. What she said is true. There is no resisting her power. Come on, I'll give you a ride back in a sulky so you can get a bit more sleep before the morning comes around. Don't worry about her anger and stuff. Kerridwen's pleased with what you've done so far. She told me herself."

.

Marji pushed the mush around his plate, eager to make sure there were no lip biters hidden in his meal. He was almost ready to decide it was safe when he noticed a telltale flash of reflection off a black nipper. He pushed his spoon down hard on it until he heard the popping sound that indicated he'd killed it. He scooped up the portion containing the dead parasite and flicked it out through the bars. "Nice try! You might want to use a smaller one next time." There was no reply. The guards must have retired early for the night, feeling confident there'd be no trouble now the men were all shackled and locked in their stalls. A scream rang out from one of the stalls to his right, telling Marji one of the men had found a lip cutter in his meal the hard way. It was a favourite sport among the guards, slipping the genetically engineered bugs into a man's dinner from time to time. They were like tiny crabs that, when placed in the mouth, would seek to escape by pinching down hard on the inside of the lip. The worst part of it wasn't so much the painful cut as the inevitable infection that would follow.

Marji scooped up a mouthful of the slop on his plate and slipped it into his mouth where he rolled it around for a while so saliva would mix with it, making it easier to digest. He peered out through the bars and wondered about the world outside, about whether the other lands were like this. He'd heard rumours about places where men and women were seen as equals, and where people moved about in mechanical carriages instead of riding on the back of slugs. A world where wrathapillars were small and almost harmless. What's the point in dreams when reality is so harsh? he thought to himself. Then they appeared, the Seer and two strangers wearing strange clothes, a boy and a girl, right here inside his stall. He sniffed his food, wondering if he may have been drugged with something that would have a telltale aroma.

The Seer looked at him and asked, "You, what's your name?"

Marji replied, "How did you get here?" He looked at Patsy and Jai. "And who are you two?"

"Hello, I'm Patsy, and this is a distant relative of mine." Jai waved as Patsy introduced him. "His name's Jai."

The Seer said, "It doesn't matter how we got here. What matters is that we need your help, and you need ours. Now, I asked you a question. I expect an answer."

Marji rubbed at the grey stubble on his chin. His grimy salt and pepper hair was tied back in a ponytail. "I'll answer your questions when you've answered mine."

The Seer took a deep breath and stared at the ground in an effort to contain her frustration.

Patsy stepped forward. "The Grand Field Commander has something that belongs to us, but we need to distract her if we're to get into her office and get it back. We figured the best way to do that would be if we helped all the males escape and stage a rebellion."

Marji laughed. "Such things take a great deal of time and planning. I still don't understand just how you've broken into my stall, and even if this is real. I'll need more proof if you're going to convince me to take you seriously.'

Without taking her eyes off Marji, Patsy lowered a hand and drew power from the Crossworlds. Marji felt compelled to hold his gaze on her as she furrowed her brow. Then she flung her arm back, sending the barred gate of the stall flying across the courtyard outside. She looked back through the opening it had created then flung her arms upward. A deafening roar of twisting metal followed as dozens of gates from other stalls were torn from their hinges and sent flying into the centre of the courtyard.

Marji's jaw dropped. "The Enchantress!" He stepped forward and went down on one knee, casting his eyes downward. "Forgive me, my name is Marji, Marji of the Seventy-Third Rank. I pledge my fealty."

Patsy put a hand on his shoulder and smiled. "I'm not the Enchantress, and I really don't want your fealty. My name is Patsy, and I come from another world and time. A world much like this in some ways, but very different in others. My mother and grandmother have sworn oaths to protect my world from evil. One day I'll take the same oath. But right now, I need to get back what the Commander has taken from us. And to do that, I really need you to draw the Commander's attention in a way that's good for you and the other men."

By now a hundred men had wandered out of their stalls in stunned silence. They gathered around Patsy and Marji.

Marji looked toward a cast iron barrier at the far end of the courtyard that would have been four times his height. "Beyond that gate are the slugs and catapults."

A guard had appeared on the top of the wall surrounding the courtyard. "They're escaping! To arms, my sisters!"

Patsy lunged in the direction of the gates with an arm extended. A ball of dancing energy flew toward the gates, pushing them into another crossworld.

Guards were rushing onto the wall. One of them stopped and called out, "The rider was right. The Enchantress is here! We must lay down our arms!"

The first guard retorted, "Your loyalty is with the realm, not some foolish, superstitious nonsense."

The second guard pointed to where slugs were now entering the courtyard. "Do you not trust your own eyes?"

The first guard took a blowpipe from her holster and sent a dart coated in wrathapillar poison into the second guard's neck. She collapsed to the ground dead. The first guard then raced to where a giant bell was suspended above the main gate to the courtyard. She leapt off the wall and grabbed the bell's chain, causing it to ring out through the city. She grimaced with pain at the deafening sound that reverberated through her head and body. Three times the metal ball on the chain struck home against the thick brass. On the third strike, it was too much for her. She released her grip then fell to the cast iron below.

Patsy lunged toward the main gate, tearing it from its hinges and sending it into a distant crossworld.

Marji and the hundred odd men looked at Patsy. Marji asked, "What now?"

Patsy said, "You lead them to freedom."

Marji looked around at the men. None of them had ever known what it meant to have hope, but he could sense something stirring in them now.

The Seer said, "You know the scriptures, do you not?"

Marji turned to her.

The Seer took a deep breath and closed her eyes as she focused on the words that she'd never thought would come to pass in her lifetime. "The Enchantress shall break the bonds of those who serve when she has become one of three. A humble beast of burden shall then rise forth and set men free that they may live as equals among the women." She walked up to him, her gaze piercing him with its intensity. "Step forth and meet your destiny, Marji of the Seventy-Fourth Rank."

He nodded, then took a step back and turned to address the others. "What say you? Do we rise?"

His question was met with a roaring approval.

He punched the air and roared as loud as he could. "Raid the armoury! Mount the slugs!"

No one noticed the Trilogy had disappeared.

·

The Grand Field Commander thundered with rage. "Let none of them escape. In the morning, I want to be there personally to see them fed to the wrathapillars."

"Of course, Commander, but what of the Seer and the Enchantress?"

"Enchantress? A girl performs a few parlour tricks, having obviously been trained by the Seer, and you fall for some superstitious claptrap?"

The sergeant at arms gestured toward Keesnah. The rider was tied by her limbs so she was spread-eagled between two columns. "And her?"

The Grand Field Commander sneered at the rider. "She won't be going anywhere. Come, we'll deal with the usurpers and then return to tease the truth out of her."

Keesnah struggled to watch the Grand Field Commander and her sergeant at arms leave through vision blurred by the bruising around her eyes. They were almost out of sight when she let out a gasp at the sight of Patsy, Jai, and the Seer appearing in the middle of the room. She prepared to call out, but the Seer held a finger to her lips then pointed at

Keesnah's mouth, compelling her to be quiet.

Patsy looked at the Seer and whispered, "That's something I haven't learned yet, how to make someone silent. I didn't even notice you draw power to do it."

The Seer replied, "That's because I didn't. I merely gave a look of authority, letting her know her interests would best be served by obeying the will of one whose power she fears."

In a hushed voice, Keesnah asked, "Why would you come to this room, like walking into the den of the hungry lion?"

"It is safe to enter the lion's den if you have first given it food to eat outside of its den, is it not?" The Seer walked over to Keesnah and began untying her bonds.

Keesnah's eyes betrayed her surprise. "You've come to set me free?"

"No, we've come for the beast of burden's metal box that is full of magical power. But I will not see someone suffer in bondage for no good reason. Did you see where the Commander left it?"

Jai scanned the room until his eyes fell upon the Grand Field Commander's desk. "No!" He raced across to inspect his phone. It had been taken from its case. The back had been removed in a clumsy manner, causing a few deep scratches. The battery had also been taken out along with the sim and memory cards. He picked up the sim and held it up. "I hope she hasn't managed to damage it."

Patsy walked across and asked, "Is that the source of its power?"

Jai pointed to the battery. "No, the power comes from the lithium battery." He then held the sim close to Patsy's face for emphasis. "This is the sim card. This is kind of what tells the phone which signal it should lock into. If this isn't working when we get to the portal, we'll never find my place and time."

Patsy stared at the bits of phone. "Can you put it back together?"

"Oh yeah." As he answered her, Jai was already halfway through reassembling the phone.

Keesnah asked, "When did you learn to speak in words rather than grunting as an animal?"

Jai stopped and turned around. "Why, I hadn't even noticed before. I can hear you as though you were speaking English."

The Seer said, "The Enchantress shared with you some of her power, that is how she saved you. It would seem some of her knowledge was shared as well." She paused before continuing. "Let's just hope you have also gained a part of her wisdom."

"How dare you!" The booming voice of the Grand Field Commander filled the room as she stood in the doorway. "Guards, seize them!"

Patsy looked at Jai, he'd just put the back on his phone. She then looked across at the Seer. "We need to go." As she spoke, a guard blew through her pipe, the dart aimed perfectly at Patsy's neck. It hit the wall as Patsy and the others disappeared.

．

Keesnah collapsed when they reappeared outside the walls. She sat up and hung her head between her bent knees as she struggled to recover from the torture she'd endured at the hands of the Commander.

Jai punched the air. "The sim's still working! Yes! We should be able to get a signal when we get back to the portal."

Keesnah looked up. "I don't understand. What sort of signal comes from a metal box that emits light? Is someone trying to contact you?"

Jai glanced across and smiled. "I can get signals and messages from people in lots of different ways. But the signal I'm talking about is like something that opens a door to them. And to get that signal, we just need to use the tracking app to find our way back to the portal."

"App? You can now speak in words rather than meaningless grunts, and yet still you use words that have no meaning."

Patsy smiled at Keesnah and offered her a hand getting to her feet. "Don't worry. I still find his metal box hard to comprehend as well." Patsy strained under the rider's weight, slipping the woman's arm over her shoulder once she was standing. She looked to the Seer then back to the rider. "You will come with us, won't you?"

Keesnah and the Seer looked at each other. The Seer nodded, then Keesnah turned to Patsy. "As the prophecies say, 'Two shall stand in defiance against the angry mob so as to facilitate the flight of the Enchantress that she may later return to set the world free.' We shall do what we can to make sure that you can go where you must. I believe in you. You truly are the one who was foretold."

"Oh, it's very sweet of you to have such faith in me. But really, I'm sure that the prophecies refer to someone else."

The Seer put an arm around Keesnah, allowing Patsy to release her hold. "It is also written of the Enchantress, 'She will be humble and deny the truth of her destiny until the day of her return.' You must go." A distant horn signalled that the city gates were opening. "The Commander's soldiers will be here soon, and they will not show you mercy."

"But won't that be the same for you?"

The Seer pushed her chest forward. "I am the Seer. The Commander may lack faith, but there are few among her armies that would dare to harm me."

Jai said, "Can't you and Keesnah just disappear if you're attacked?" He turned to Patsy. "Can't we all do that? There's no reason to leave them behind. They can come with us."

Patsy thought back to the admonishment they'd received from Krinkle-myst. "No, we can't."

"Why? Because some wood-elf got angry with you?" He gestured toward Keesnah and the Seer. "Their lives are at stake."

Patsy turned away to hide her tears. "I'm sorry…"

The Seer placed a hand on Jai's shoulder. "The Enchantress speaks the truth."

Jai pushed the hand away. "We can surely at least take them to the portal with us… do that thing of just letting ourselves be there."

The Seer shook her head. "I have no strength left to summon the power to do so. Such things take a great deal from one."

He turned to Patsy.

"I've drawn lots of power setting the men free. I want to save what strength I still have for if we need it."

"But you draw it from the Crossworlds."

"Do you think that's a trivial thing? I threw giant metal gates into other worlds with no knowledge of where they might fall. And every bit of power I draw comes from somewhere else. Do you know what the ramifications are for the worlds where it's come from? I don't. And if you think it's easy to draw that power, then think again. I'm tired. I don't know that I even have the strength to allow myself to be somewhere else right now."

Jai's jaw hung open. "I'm sorry. I just thought—"

"No, you didn't think, that's the problem." She was gulping for breath as tears streamed down her face. "All you seem to think about is what suits you. Do you have any idea what it's like to be me? What do you expect of me? You and everyone else, you all expect things of me. Do you think I asked for this? Do you think I actually wanted to be cast as someone who has to protect the world? And now, I'm apparently the

Enchantress!" She turned away from the now silent group. "I just want to go home and enjoy my studies with Miss Jenkins."

"There they are!" The call came from up above. A scout was mounted on a giant dragonfly swooping low so it was passing between the trees of mint. They could feel the wind of beating wings as it flew ahead of them. The dragonfly's pilot lifted a megaphone and looked over her shoulder, calling the advancing ground troops to action. "Fire at will!"

"Go now, run!" said the Seer.

"We can't leave you," said Jai.

Keesnah pleaded with him, "Just go, protect the Enchantress."

Patsy straightened up and grabbed Jai's arm. "They're right, we need to go." She looked at the rider. "I'll come back for you."

"I have no doubt that you will come back. It has been foretold. But now, Enchantress, you must go!"

Feeling uncomfortable with the burden of being labelled as the 'Enchantress,' Patsy asked, "Please, could you just call me Patsy?"

The air around them was filled by the whistling of flying darts. One dart found the Seer's sandal, missing her flesh by a finger width.

Jai looked up and pointed to the northeast. "The portal's that way. If we run, we can be there in a few minutes." He looked up. "The battery's getting low. If it runs out, we'll never find our way there."

The dragonfly was circling high above them. "Fire the catapults!"

Patsy grabbed Jai's arm, dragging him in the direction of the portal. "Come on then, let's go."

As they ran into the jungle of mint, Keesnah called out, "May speed be on your side, Enchantress... Patsy."

Wrathapillars fired from the catapults were landing all around Keesnah and the Seer. Seeing the Dragonfly change its course in an effort to follow Patsy and Jai, the Seer reached down and focused what strength she had left in drawing energy from the Crossworlds. The dragonfly was almost out of sight when she flung her arm skyward. The massive burst of energy she unleashed pushed the giant insect off its course and knocked the pilot off its back.

Keesnah and the Seer looked at each other as another rain of darts came down around them. Keesnah pulled one from her shoulder while the Seer had to pull one from her leg. The advancing soldiers emerged from the green fog with blowpipes ready for another attack. Keesnah and the Seer looked into each other's eyes and recited a line of the prophecy together. "And the two gave their lives that the Enchantress might survive and hence return in future times to free the people from tyranny."

.

Patsy and Jai could hear the fallen pilot calling out through her megaphone. "I will find you, Enchantress. You might as well accept your fate."

Jai looked in the direction of the sound. "What the—" He turned back to Patsy. "Didn't we see her fall from that thing she was riding?"

"I guess the mint must have broken her fall."

The megaphone echoed through the forest. "There is no escape. We know this forest better than you."

Jai said, "I think she's bluffing."

"How far away is the portal now?"

Jai looked at his phone. Colour drained from his features as the screen went blank. "The battery."

"The what?"

"The battery, it's dead. It's got no more power."

"Can you remember where it said the portal is?"

"Not well enough to be confident."

The hollow tone of the megaphone was getting closer. "I will find you."

Patsy reached out. "Give me the phone."

"Why?"

"Just give it to me." Patsy snatched the phone away from him then held it down low as she closed her eyes and concentrated until it was consumed in a glowing ball of energy. She relaxed and the glow subsided. She opened her eyes and handed the phone back to Jai. "Try it now."

"That's just great. It's probably fried now. We'll be stuck here."

"Just try it!"

The megaphone was getting louder. "I can hear you. Don't move. If you don't attempt another escape, your lives may be spared."

Feeling his heartbeat quicken, Jai had little choice but to trust that Patsy's attempt at charging the phone had worked. He pressed the power button. "I can't believe it. It's working!"

"Where's the map?"

"It's got to finish booting up first."

They started running in the direction they'd been heading before.

Still, the megaphone got closer. "They're escaping. Fire at them on sight."

A dart whistled past Patsy's ear. "How long does that take?"

"It's almost there." With his eyes fixed on the phone, Jai tripped on a fallen mint branch, sending the phone flying from his hands. It was just as well. A dart sped through the air where his neck would have otherwise been. The wind was knocked out of him as he hit the ground.

A robotic voice came from the device. "You are three minutes from your destination." Patsy went down on the ground to try and avoid what was now a shower of darts. She crawled through the slime and mud of the forest floor to grab the phone then scrambled back to Jai. The slime that now matted her hair and covered the front of her dress stank. She lay next to Jai and held the phone up to him. "Which way?" Still too winded to talk, he raised a finger and pointed.

"Gotcha!"

Patsy looked up and saw the pilot standing over them, bringing a blowpipe to her lips. Patsy wrapped an arm around Jai and allowed her mind to blend with his. He put up no resistance. She found the part of his mind that understood where the phone had told him the portal was located.

The pilot blew in her pipe. The dart embedded itself in the ground where Patsy and Jai had been.

*

Patsy was passed out when Jai came to, brought back to his senses by the now distant megaphone.

"I will find you. Your parlour tricks will not stop me."

He looked at the pool of thick green slime they'd been transported to. The large rock on the other side confirmed that Patsy had brought them to the right place.

He put a hand on her shoulder and gave it a little shake. There was no response. He bent down and checked she was still breathing. While there was still breath, it was shallow. He grabbed his phone and went through the contacts until he found his mother and called her. After three rings he heard a recorded message: "Hi, you've called Glenda. I'm either unavailable, or don't want to talk to you. Leave a message if you want, but I probably won't bother getting back to you." He shook his head. *Yep, that's Mum alright.*

The megaphone was getting closer again. "I know you're going to the slime pool. You can't fool me."

Jai tried calling his grandmother. Come on, pick up, Nan. It rang once... twice... three times.

The megaphone was getting closer. "I'm almost there. You might as well give up. We've got you surrounded now."

Come on Nan, Jai looked at Patsy. This is my fault. I never should have done this.

The ringing stopped. "Hello? Jai?"

"Nan! Thank God you answered. Are you at home?"

"Is that really you?" Her voice sounded more fragile than usual, huskier.

"Of course it's me. Just tell me, are you at home? I need you to open the portal."

"Where have you been?"

"I went to get help, remember?"

"But that was so long ago." Jai's Nan paused, then let out a little sob before continuing. "Your mother gave up on ever seeing you again."

"I've only been gone a few days."

"It's been almost fifteen years—"

"Nan, I need you to open the portal, now!"

"I never gave up—"

Jai looked up and saw two dragonflies circling overhead. "Nan, please! Where are you?"

"I'm sitting by the pool at the creek. I'm reading a wonderful book by—"

At least she was right there. There was still hope. "Nan, this is life or death, I need you to open the portal."

"Oh, well you should have said so earlier. Hold on a minute. I'll have it open for you in a jiffy."

"I've got no time to lose, Nan. I'm going to start moving into the water, and I'm going to trust that you can get it to open in time. I'm bringing Patricia McIntyre with me."

"That's nice, dear."

"I'm going to put you on speaker phone while I carry her into the portal."

"Oh, that's lovely that you don't want her feet to get wet."

Jai didn't bother replying. Nan had always been sharp and quick-witted in the past. It broke his heart to hear her sounding this way. He scooped up Patsy and placed the phone on her belly so he'd still be able to communicate with his Nan as he worked his way into the portal.

"This is your last chance to stop."

Jai looked over his shoulder and saw the pilot raising a blowpipe to her lips. He was knee-deep now in the pool, the stench of the slime assaulting his nostrils as he stirred it up. A dart whistled past his ear. "Come on, Nan. Please—"

"Just trying to remember the words, dear. It's been a long time, you know."

Another dart whistled past. The slime was starting to come to life, moving around him and becoming shallower in his immediate vicinity. *Thank you, Nan.*

More soldiers appeared on the bank with blowpipes. Then, Jai heard a thud. He looked over his shoulder and saw the pilot fall to the ground with a huge gash on his forehead where he'd been hit by a rock. There was a veritable sea of rocks flying out of the forest and taking down soldiers. Marji stepped forward and called out, "Go! Get the Enchantress to safety."

CHAPTER 5

The slimy water swirled around Jai as he carried the unconscious Patsy into the portal. In amongst the thundering sounds of the vortex he heard a woman gasp. Looking over his shoulder he saw the shimmering ghost-like images of Neridah, Meredith, and the Reverend. Meredith had her hands against her cheeks and was struggling to breathe on seeing her daughter look so lifeless.

"This way, laddie," said the Reverend. "Time to bring her home. Then we can send you back to your time and nurse her back to health to do what must be done."

Jai looked at Patsy's face, then looked in the direction he'd been heading. The water was becoming clearer, and he could see his Nan waiting for him on the bank of the pool. He turned back to the Trinity. "No, she needs to help me find my sister and get the Book of Wisdom back first."

Neridah's phantom image stamped its foot. "Jai! That's wrong and it's selfish! She needs help, help that you won't be able to give her. Bring her back, now!"

Meredith was crying. She reached out. "Please, Jai, please bring my baby back to me."

The Reverend stabbed a finger in Jai's direction. "We put ourselves into the void to help you. We did that to provide you with a beacon to find your way back to the right place and time. We trusted that you would come back and then pull us free of the void. What you're proposing is a betrayal of that trust."

Jai said, "I'm sorry. This is what I have to do." He turned his back on the Trinity and made his way toward his Nan.

·

"Well, that didn't go well." Neridah avoided eye contact with the other two.

Meredith replied, "I'm not surprised. A little disappointed, but not surprised."

"I expected better of the boy," said the Reverend, his eyes cast low.

Neridah glared at him. "Oh? What, because he looks like you? Do you expect him to do what you believe he should do just to please you? Would you have behaved any differently at that age? How's it feel to see yourself in the mirror? Are you comfortable with what you see?"

"Mother, that's enough. We're stuck in this void until Patricia can pull us out. Jai's made his decision, and we have no choice but to live with it. Even if that means we're stuck in this situation for weeks on end." An uncomfortable silence ensued as the reality of Meredith's statement sank in.

*

Gladys doubled over as she coughed, gagging as she took in another deep breath of the putrid smoke-filled air. It reeked of sulphur and bile. She was drenched in sweat and wondered how long her decrepit body would cope. Most other Nasqa would have departed the body by now, seeking an escape to a different crossworld. But not this one. This one had learned to enjoy the pain and suffering of the host's body. Let her feel it, while I revel in her agony. And besides, this was a different timeline. The Nasqa had no familiarity with what worlds lay nearby so likely wouldn't be able to access other crossworlds without some sort of assistance.

A gust of wind drew her attention. She turned and saw a shaft of light with swirling flames around it. The portal—that's where the portal must be. It's opened!

She ran toward it, not caring as her dress caught fire. There's a pathway out of this inferno. As she neared the swirling tornado of fire, she could sense it was retracting, as though getting ready to close. She threw herself forward, diving in as it snapped shut. Gladys Taylor disappeared with it.

*

Destellie sang as she washed her clothes in the creek. It was a chore she loathed, but she found singing made it more bearable.

Felibrey's voice from behind caused her to jump. "Your singing is so sweet it puts the birds to shame."

She turned and forced a smile. "It's only so sweet because it's a song I learned from them. The magpies are quite generous in sharing their knowledge of songs and melodies." She put her washing aside and turned to face where he sat on a rock next to her. They shared a morning kiss and embraced, moving their chins to rest on each other's shoulders. "You slept late."

"Yes, but I feel much better for it." They relaxed their embrace before Felibrey asked, "Have you seen the Reverend this morning? He was supposed to show me how to fix the roof shingles in place. But he never returned from the McIntyre's last night."

"I wouldn't worry. It's not unusual for him to stay the night there."

"Yes, but when he does, he normally returns early."

Destellie looked up and listened to a magpie warbling in a tree. It sang a song about the freshness of worms collected after rain. She wondered as she listened whether any of the local wildlife would betray her deception. "Felibrey, have you ever thought that maybe we'd be better moving to Sydney, or another place? Maybe even the goldfields?"

"But that would be breaking the promise we made to the Reverend."

"Did we? Did we ever really make a promise to him? Maybe we should think about the promise we're preparing to make to each other. Maybe we should start a new life, away from where anyone we know might find us."

·

Nan stared at Jai. "How is it that you haven't aged?"

"I told you on the phone. To me, I've only been gone a few days."

Nan looked at Patsy's limp form as Jai lowered her to the sandy part of the bank. "Oh my. This doesn't look good."

Jai's voice was soft. "Her breathing is shallow."

Nan closed her eyes as she passed a hand over Patsy. "She's exhausted herself. She needs sleep more than anything else, and a good bath. She'll likely catch a cold if she stays in those putrid wet rags much longer. We can't risk that with the weak state she's in." She looked up at Jai. "So, this really is Patricia McIntyre?"

Jai ignored the question. He was more interested in how the woman he'd last seen a few days ago had aged so much. "How long did you say I've been gone?"

Nan sighed. "Almost fifteen years."

He could see all those years and more etched into Nan's face as he explored the deep lines that told a tale of sadness and loss. So different from the face he was familiar with that had lit up the world of his youth with happiness and joy. "I'm so sorry, Nan." He went to give her a hug only to be pushed away.

Nan pulled her head as far from him as she could, pinching her nose at the same time. "We need to get you and this young lady up to the house and get you both cleaned up. We can hug and chat all you want later." She picked up her book and started up the steps. Jai marvelled at how, apart from a good deal of wear, the pathway hadn't changed since Patsy's grandfather had first cut the stairway out of the sandstone. Nan turned and glared back at him. "Come on then." She looked him up and down. "That shower isn't going to come to you."

Jai put his phone in his pocket and squatted down in readiness to pick up Patsy again. He was just starting to slip his arms under her when a pair of pixies appeared. They fluttered above Patsy, inspecting her. Having not encountered them before, Jai leaned back to try to create a safe distance between them. "What the—"

Bandah looked up and said, "What the what? What's your name kid, and what are you doing bringing Patsy into this timeline?"

"I..." Jai couldn't get the words out.

On hearing the pixie's voice, Nan stopped and turned around.

"Bandah?"

Talia landed on Patsy's cheek and lifted an eyelid. "She'll be okay. Just needs a little laughter to bring her smile back."

Bandah turned away from Jai and asked Talia, "A bit of tickle therapy perhaps?"

Talia nodded. "Yep, unless you can think of another way to make someone laugh in their sleep."

Bandah positioned himself just under Patsy's chin then started beating his wings against her neck. A few seconds later, a giggle escaped her lips. Talia joined Bandah in the exercise, causing Patsy's eyes to open wide as she burst into a fit of laughter. "Oh, I'm laughing too much. I can't breathe. Stop it." She started to swat at her neck with her hands. "Please, stop it!"

Satisfied their job was done, Bandah and Talia drew their wings back in while Patsy took in a few deep breaths. She looked at the pixies and asked, "What was that for? What are you even doing here?"

Bandah replied, "You're asking us what we're doing here? Are you even aware of where you are?"

Patsy looked around. "I'm home." She looked up at Jai and smiled. "We made it." She looked across at Nan and asked, "Who are you? Where's Mother and Nana-Neri?"

Jai gestured towards Nan. "Patsy, meet Nan. Nan, meet Patsy."

Bandah said, "You still haven't told us who you are, kid."

Nan said, "Well, Bandah, if you and Talia had bothered to check in on me anytime in the past thirty-five years, you'd know that this is my grandson, Jai."

Talia asked Nan, "So, where's Glenda?" She cast a quick glance at Bandah. "She always was a little cutie."

The lines in Nan's face seemed to deepen as she responded. "We don't talk anymore."

"What do you mean?" asked Jai. "Where is Mum? I tried to call her when we first reached the portal, but she wouldn't answer."

"She didn't take it well when you didn't come back. With the Nasqa having taken Melanie, and you seemingly lost forever after entering the portal, she decided to devote herself to trying to find your sister. She reformed her band and uses touring as a means of trying to locate her… and to finance the search."

"The Crimson Dockers are back together?"

Nan nodded. "It's the worst thing she could have done. I never did approve of how she used her magic to make that band stand out. And as for the other band members…"

"Has she had any luck finding Mel?"

"Yes, just recently. She's being held by the Nasqa somewhere in Sydney, so your mother's based herself there now so she can pinpoint exactly where." Nan looked at Patsy. She was shivering and her teeth were chattering. "Come on, let's get you up to the house for a shower. I'll see if I can find something you can wear while we wash your dress." She turned to the pixies. "Are you two going to join us?"

"Absolutely," replied Bandah. He landed on Jai's shoulder. "And you, young man, are going to answer my questions as we head up there."

"We can't leave the portal yet," said Patsy. "My family, they're trapped in the void. Mother, Nana-Neri, and the Reverend, they formed a Trilogy and entered the void to help Jai and I find our way back to my timeline. They can't get out of there without my help, and I can only do that from there. They're stuck until I get back."

Bandah and Talia looked at each other. "That's not good," said Bandah.

Talia replied, "I'll go and let them know what's happening. With a bit of luck, Mrs Smith and I might be able to team up to peel back the veil to the void enough to pull them out."

"You can't, though, it's a different timeline. We don't belong there, just like Patsy doesn't belong here in this one."

"Have you got a better idea?"

Bandah thought about it. His answer was soft, almost inaudible. "No. Just be careful not to connect with yourself while you're there."

Patsy asked, "I don't understand, how will you find the right timeline... there's so many?"

"The void intersects them all. That's why it's so dangerous to be trapped in there." Talia turned to Bandah. "I know it's a long shot, but I've got to give it a try."

.

Colin grabbed his flintlock and walked out to the veranda when he heard the sound of the approaching horses. His heart sank at the sight of Captain Taylor and six other soldiers, no doubt all controlled by Nasqa. "Captain Taylor, I can't say that it's a pleasure to see you."

"Nor I, you murdering bastard."

"I beg your pardon."

Captain Taylor glanced across at the rider next to him. "Arrest this man and clap him in irons." He turned back to Colin. "This time I promise, you will hang."

Clara Jenkins and Cook raced onto the veranda as one soldier took Colin's flintlock and the other attached irons to his wrists and ankles. Clara looked at Colin and asked, "What's happening?"

Colin was silent.

She turned to Captain Taylor. "What's the meaning of this?" As she watched the Captain and his men, she noticed their shadows followed different movements and represented creatures just as ghastly as those in Gladys Taylor's shadow. She turned her attention to the captain. "What is he accused of?"

"He is guilty of the murder of my wife. Her sulky was found abandoned down the road, and her footprints led to this property."

Cook tried to reach out to Colin but was pushed back by one of the soldiers. "Don't you worry, Mr McIntyre, sir. I'll go and talk to Vincent, he'll know what to do."

Captain Taylor laughed. "Mr Donaldson won't be much help to you." As he spoke, another soldier rode into the property, leading Gladys Taylor's sulky. Vincent Donaldson was in the seat, weighed down by the chains on his wrists and ankles. There was a large gash over his closed and blackened right eye. "My poor wife's sulky and horse were found on Mr Donaldson's property. He is clearly an accessory to the fact. I intend to see the two of them hang side by side."

Cook burst into tears. "Please, God, please, please tell me this isn't happening." Cook started to sway, and then her knees gave way. Clara caught her before she collapsed, struggling to hold the woman's weight.

"We'll go down to Sydney. We'll take this to the governor if we have to."

Captain Taylor's laughter grew louder. "Oh, please do."

Jimmy and Darcy O'Sullivan ran across from the stables. Jimmy called out, "Oi! What in the name of God is goin' on here?"

Captain Taylor turned to one of his soldiers and said, "If that man utters another word, I want you to shoot him." The soldier smiled as he lifted a pistol and pointed it in Jimmy's direction. Jimmy stopped running, his mouth hanging open. Darcy continued up to the veranda to help Clara support Cook.

•

Gladys emerged from the stinking pool of swirling slime. The soggy remains of her dress and petticoat were blackened and hung from her wiry frame like lichen. Darts covered in wrathapillar poison whistled through the air around her, some striking her, some striking the myriad other creatures that had taken advantage of the portal opening in countless worlds scattered across different timelines. There were giant rodents, griffins, fairies, and other creatures Gladys couldn't recognise. Someone had been careless when they'd opened this portal, allowing a chaos of creatures who had no place in this crossworld or timeline to come flooding in. Gladys smiled. She liked chaos.

Feeling her leg muscles weakening from the impact of the poison darts, the Nasqa within Gladys let go. The life drained from her as she fell to the ground. The hint of a smile on her face suggested there was somehow a final moment of peace, an uncomfortable end to a life spent seeking empowerment through being controlled by another. The Nasqa swept through the air and through the minds of the soldiers on the bank as it sought a new host, searching for a mind that displayed weak character. Then it found a mind that had all the traits it was looking for. Disregard for what mattered and a willingness to change one's values to suit the occasion.

The Nasqa that had once inhabited Sean O'Malley, then Gladys Taylor, now took control of the Grand Field Commander.

•

Patsy was stunned by how the library was the same now as it had been a hundred and fifty years ago. The only noticeable difference? The Book of Wisdom was nowhere to be seen. She stood at its empty stand.

"Please, do sit down," said Nan.

Patsy looked around and saw that Nan had taken a seat at the main desk where her father normally sat and was gesturing for Jai and herself to take seats across from her. She hesitated before taking tentative steps toward the desk.

Jai had already taken a seat. "What's wrong?" he asked.

Patsy seemed oblivious to his presence. "It feels so weird. I'm being treated as a guest in my own home." It didn't help that she was wearing clothes unlike any she'd worn before. And that shower... the hot beads of water raining down on her, cleaning away the grime of another world. That, in itself, was as strange and frightening as anything she'd experienced during this new adventure.

"Of course it does," said Nan. "This must be very difficult for you."

Patsy nodded in response, then glanced at Jai. "I'm sorry, I didn't realise. It must have been like this for you, too, when you arrived."

"Not really," said Jai. "Mum used to drag me and Mel around on tour all the time. I've spent most of my life living out of a suitcase. I'd been around the world twice by the time I was ten. It was only when Mel got taken that she stopped touring and broke up the band."

"What's this 'band' that you keep talking about?"

"The Crimson Dockers? Punk and grunge rediscovered with a touch of alternative folk for good measure. Mum wrote every lyric and note of every song."

"That's not helping me."

"Perhaps this will help." Nan powered up her tablet then opened a page promoting the Crimson Dockers' next gig. "The Crimson Dockers are playing at the Sydney Opera House tomorrow night." She looked at Jai. "Your mother always sends me two tickets and backstage passes. I've never used them, but I think you two need to go down there for this one."

Jai asked, "Will you come with us?"

Nan sighed. "No. There's only two tickets." A tear started to well up in the corner of her eye and her voice became shaky. "But even if there were three, I really don't think I could—"

Seeing her distress, Jai raced around the desk and threw his arms around Nan. She buried her head in his shoulder and sobbed.

.

As the sulky entered Springwood Barracks, Colin noticed something very different from the last time he'd entered the compound a year earlier. This time, every face looked toward him with contempt. This time, every soldier was clearly Nasqa.

He looked at the gallows that were under construction. It occurred to him that this time would be different. This time there wasn't even going to be a trial. He looked across at Vincent and found himself lost for words. Meredith, Neridah, and the Reverend were trapped in limbo in an effort to bring back his lost daughter. For the first time in his life, Colin McIntyre could see no hope of salvation.

CHAPTER 6

Patsy had always wanted to ride on a train. She'd never dreamed that the first time she did so it would be powered by electricity rather than steam. The bra that Nan had insisted she had to wear felt uncomfortable, but she liked the t-shirt with its image of a sultry looking Stevie Nicks, the word 'Witch' scrawled across the top in red. Nan had bought her the shirt during their morning shopping escapade. She was still trying to get used to the feel of the jeans and struggled to understand how something with several tears in it could be sold as 'new.'

"Just wait until you see the Opera House. That will seriously blow your mind," said Jai.

Why is he taking so much joy in this? Patsy really didn't like the side of Jai she was seeing now. Almost every minute since she'd arrived in this time had been an overload of new concepts and ideas to absorb, and

Jai seemed to take pleasure in watching her struggle to take it all in.

"There it is." Jai was pointing out the window to the most unusual building Patsy had ever seen. But what amazed her more was the bridge they were crossing and the size of the buildings behind the Opera House. She wondered what could possibly be contained within those structures. What purpose did they serve? She opened her mouth to ask, but then decided it might just lead to even greater confusion.

·

The crisp winter morning was filled with a symphony of bird songs. A few soldiers were up and about to watch Colin and Vincent being marched to the gallows.

No words were spoken as the nooses were secured around their necks.

Colin looked across at Vincent with his swollen and blackened eye. He felt gratitude for everything Vincent had done to support him and his family. He also felt an overwhelming sense of guilt. Vincent had never even met Gladys. He had no real connection to the issues that caused Captain Taylor to be so full of hate. He opened his mouth to say something, to express his sorrow. To confess his culpability for what was about to befall them. His jaw hung limp; He could find no words.

A lever was pulled.

Captain Taylor smiled then walked away as Colin McIntyre and Vincent Donaldson's lives came to an end.

·

Patsy scanned the orchestra members then turned to Jai and whispered, "Which one is her?"

Jai laughed. "This is just the orchestra, the backup musicians. Mum will be out soon enough. And trust me, you'll know it's her when she appears. She looks a lot like your grandmother."

The melody the orchestra was playing started to change, becoming a repetitious string of a few bars.

The audience saw it as a sign that the band was preparing to start and, at the end of each repetition, they chanted, "Crimson!"

"What are they saying?" asked Patsy. "Is it meant to be some sort of incantation?"

"Not really, they're calling for the band to come out and start playing."

"But the orchestra is already playing."

The crowd began stomping their feet with each repetition of the chant.

Jai laughed, "You ain't seen nothing yet, Pats."

Patsy looked away and crossed her arms, disappointed by the lack of substance in Jai's answer. The chant of the crowd was getting so loud that it started to hurt her ears. Then the room went dark and the loudest sound Patsy had ever heard filled the auditorium as a spot of light focused on the woman strutting onto the stage holding a guitar.

The crowd erupted and got to their feet.

Patsy stared at the close-up images on large screens behind the stage. She placed a hand on Jai's shoulder and yelled in his ear, "She looks like Nana-Neri!"

Jai smiled.

Glenda Williams strummed the guitar again then threw her arm out at the audience as she yelled out, "Hey there, Sydney. Are you ready to rock?"

The crowd roared, "YES!"

"I didn't hear you. ARE YOU READY TO ROCK?"

"YES!"

Patsy watched in stunned awe as Glenda dropped her right hand, strumming the guitar before reaching into the Crossworlds to draw power. A dancing ball of energy built up around her hand. Patsy turned to Jai. "What's she doing?"

Jai shrugged his shoulders. "She's building the suspense."

Glenda yelled to the audience. "We are the Crimson Dockers and we are here to rock your world!" She threw her arm forward and released the ball of energy. It exploded above the crowd. The stage lit up and the band swung into the first number, "Refrained Power."

Patsy asked Jai, "Why would she use her power that way?"

"That's part of what draws people to the shows."

"But where's the danger?"

"What are you talking about? There's no danger. It's just entertainment."

"But the consequences… that power comes from elsewhere. You know that!"

Patsy chose not to say anything more and tried to make out what Glenda was singing.

> *If you knew what I can do*
> *You'd think it can't be true*
> *I hold back*
> *You don't know*
> *Hidden power*
> *Desperate needs*
> *If you knew you'd get on your knees*
> *Don't you know how it's been for me?*
> *Refrained Power!*

She held the microphone out to the audience. The crowd sang out in unison, "Refrained Power!" Patsy was shocked when she realised she'd been swept up in the chorus and was singing along herself.

Glenda took a step back as the lead guitarist ran toward the front of the stage then went down on his knees, momentum carrying him forward as his fingertips danced along the fret board. As Patsy tried to follow the movement of his hands, she noticed something disturbing… the shadows. She looked around the stage to the other band members. How could Glenda spend so much time with these people and not know? Patsy nudged Jai with her elbow. He ignored her, continuing to shake his head wildly in time with the music. She grabbed hold of him with both hands and shook him until he stopped. She yelled into his ear, struggling to be heard over the amplified music and the roar of the crowd: "Look at them!"

"Who?"

Patsy pointed to the band members. "Don't you see it?"

"What?"

"Their shadows. They're moving differently."

"That's the light show."

"What?"

"Look, there's lights flashing on and off and swinging around everywhere."

"The shadows, they're moving."

Jai pointed to the lighting grid. "The lights are moving."

"It's not just the lights."

Jai shook his head. "It's just a light show."

"They're Nasqa."

"It's a light show." Patsy's glare told him she wasn't convinced. "My mum's a witch." Patsy's expression didn't change. "Wouldn't she know if they're Nasqa?"

Patsy crossed her arms and sat down. They had seats at the front of a side box near the stage. As she watched Glenda's performance, Patsy pondered how she felt about meeting this woman whose use of magic was so careless. How would Krinkle-myst feel about this woman? It made her appreciate how much she'd learned about the importance of thinking before using magic herself.

•

Jai pulled out his phone and showed the security guard his backstage pass. The guard laughed when he looked at the fifteen-year-old device. "Hey kid, it's a wonder that antique even works. Very retro, dude." He looked across at Patsy. "Where's yours?"

Jai answered for her. "She doesn't have one."

"Is that so?"

"A phone… she doesn't have one. I've got both our tickets on mine." He swiped to reveal the second pass. "See?"

"Yeah, well, you know what, this party's no place for kids anyway—"

"Don't you realise who I am?" Jai shoved his phone in the guard's face. "See who issued the ticket? I'm her son."

"Sorry kid, even if you are, the rules are the rules. No under eighteens allowed."

Patsy asked Jai, "Where do we need to go?"

Jai pointed past the guard to a room down the corridor filled with music and laughter. "The backstage party's in there."

Patsy grabbed Jai's arm. "Okay, well let's go."

The security guard staggered back a few steps and clutched his chest hoping it might slow the sudden increase in his heart rate. He'd been talking to a couple of young teenagers, he was sure of it. But now, there was no one there. He grabbed his walkie talkie, wondering if he should call the guard inside the party to see if anyone matching their description was inside, then thought better of it. He needed this job, and he was already on his last warning after having been caught drinking on the job in the past. The last thing he wanted now was to give his superiors reason to question his sobriety.

·

"Jai?" Glenda took a step closer and reached out to touch her son's face. She didn't dare blink in case it might cause him to vanish. "Oh my God, it really is you." She burst into tears as she threw her arms around him. "I thought I'd lost you."

Jai cried, too, as he responded in kind to his mother's embrace. "I promised you I'd come back."

Glenda struggled to get the words out through her tears. "Yes, you did. My beautiful boy. But that was so long ago. I'm so sorry Jai... I'd given up hope." Glenda relaxed her grip then noticed his companion. She studied Patsy's face, moving her head around as she scanned every detail. "You're her, aren't you?" Before Patsy had a chance to respond, Glenda turned back to her son. "I can't believe it, you succeeded! You brought back Patricia McIntyre." Again, she threw her arms around her son and cried into his shoulder. "How could I have been so foolish as to give up on you?"

"It's okay, Mum, it's been quite a journey."

"I've felt so guilty all these years. I'm so sorry."

"No, I'm the one who should be sorry."

"You've been gone fifteen years, but haven't aged a bit."

Jai thought to himself, *You look like crap, Mum, what have you been doing to yourself?* He took a step back and said, "You look great yourself, Mum."

Seeing through his deception, she bit her lower lip and nodded. She pulled her son toward her then gave him another hug. "I should never have risked losing you. It was the most stupid thing I've ever done." She released her hold on him and offered her hand to Patsy. "I am so pleased to meet you, Patricia. I've read so much about you."

Patsy looked at Glenda's outstretched hand and wasn't sure how to respond. She raised her own but didn't make contact with Glenda's. Seeing Patsy's discomfort with the procedure, Glenda instead threw her arms around her. "Stuff the handshakes, you're family." Patsy couldn't help but smile at the genuine warmth she felt in Glenda's embrace. There was more she had in common with Neridah than just her appearance. Glenda took a step back and looked over her shoulder to the rest of the people enjoying the feast and drinks at the backstage party. "We really should join them for a while. Some of them paid a lot of money to attend this party, and I really need to meet and greet as many as I can before we go."

Jai asked, "Do you mind if Patsy and I just sit back here and wait for you to be finished?"

"No way! Come and join the party. You and Patricia need to meet the band."

Jai glanced across at Patsy, his expression betraying his disappointment.

Patsy thought about the disturbing shadows she'd seen cast by the band members. She forced a smile and said, "I'd really like to meet them. Thank you."

Having absorbed so many new things throughout the day, Patsy felt like she was walking through a dream as they navigated their way through the party. She'd never seen so much food laid out on tables before, even when her parents had entertained for dozens of guests on special occasions. Then, she saw the guitarist, and watched his shadow harass the young woman he was talking to. Patsy grabbed Glenda's arm. "He's Nasqa!"

"Well, duh…" Glenda rolled her eyes and sighed, waving her hand in a manner that suggested she found it tedious to have to explain what was so obvious to her. Seeing the look of confusion in Patsy's expression, Glenda softened her tone and whispered into Patsy's ear. "Keep your friends close, and your enemies closer."

Patsy stepped back and shook her head. "This is wrong."

"Is it?" Glenda put her hands on Patsy's shoulders and looked into her eyes. She spoke slowly, as though she were speaking to someone with a poor understanding of English. "I'm trying to find my daughter."

Feeling patronised, Patsy took another step back to take her shoulders beyond Glenda's reach. "What you do on stage, that's wrong, too."

"Excuse me?" Glenda paused before asking, "Are you casting judgement on me?"

Patsy shot back, "I don't need to. You know it's wrong."

"Huh?" Glenda turned to Jai. "Do you understand any of this?"

Jai took a deep breath before responding. "Umm… after what I've seen in the past few days, I think it might be worthwhile listening to her."

Unimpressed by her son's response, Glenda turned back to Patsy. "Now, you listen to me. I've spent fifteen years putting this plan into place—"

A tall man with an effeminate voice came up behind Glenda and put his arms around her. "When are you going to join the party? Your fans await. They've paid top dollar for a piece of you—" He froze mid-sentence, as did the rest of the room.

Patsy's breathing was short and her arms were outstretched. Glenda glared at her. "A time freeze? You've done a time freeze?"

"On everyone in the room but us."

Glenda's words were barely audible. "And you did it without even reciting a spell?"

"I don't need words when I'm angry."

Glenda held up her arms in an effort to somehow shield the room from Patsy. "Whatever you're thinking of doing, please don't. I've spent too much time setting this up."

"You've spent fifteen years drawing energy from other worlds for no reason. You've been pandering to the Nasqa." Patsy stepped around Glenda and approached the lead guitarist. "I'll show you how to deal with a mind thief."

The guitarist's eyes widened. The Nasqa possessing him struggled to break free of the time freeze. "Please, not the void, anything but that!"

"Oh, so you know who I am?"

"Every Nasqa knows about your sadistic madness, how could we not?"

Patsy reached into the musician's chest and ripped out the Nasqa, then held it up high. "Tell me where she is, or so help me, you'll be spread across a hundred unattached realms in the void."

Detached from the musician's body, the Nasqa had to communicate using its thoughts. *I can't...*

Patsy reached down with her free hand and opened a connection to the void. "Are you sure about that?"

Please... I can't... the consequences...

Patsy pushed part of the Nasqa into the void then slammed the opening shut, leaving part of the Nasqa lost for eternity. "Are the consequences as bad as what you're facing now?" Patsy opened another connection to the void. "Last chance." She started moving the Nasqa toward the void.

No... I'll tell you. Just please, promise me you'll help me get to somewhere I can be safe.

The Nasqa controlling the drummer broke free of the time freeze, just enough to call out, "Don't do it. Don't be a fool." His face screwed up in a sneer. "You know what happens to traitors."

Patsy turned to Glenda and extended the hand that held the shadowy apparition of the Nasqa. "Here, hold this."

"What?" Glenda took a step back.

"Just grab hold of it, with your mind as well as your hand."

"Eww!" Glenda looked at Patsy and asked, "Are you for real?"

Jai stepped forward. "I'll hold it for you."

"You're not strong enough. She needs to."

Glenda protested, "This is madness."

"Just take it."

Glenda took a tentative step forward and reached out, wrapping her right hand around the Nasqa. As soon as Patsy released her hold on the shadowy form it started thrashing about like an eel on the end of a fishing line. "Whoah!" Glenda brought up her other hand and tightened her grip.

Patsy walked over to the drummer and ripped the Nasqa from his chest. "So, you think you're stronger than him?"

That one's always been weak.

"You don't fear the void?"

I don't fear anything.

Patsy tore the Nasqa in two, throwing one half into the void.

You'll never find the girl, nor your precious little book. It's ours now.

She threw the other half into the void as well, not caring whether or not it would be able to reconnect with the other part of itself.

Glenda was still struggling to hold the Nasqa. When Patsy approached, it broke free and was gone. Patsy looked around and saw the bass player. His long hair was halfway down his back and looked like it hadn't been washed in a long time. His beard was just as long and dirty. His eyes darted back and forth as he tried to break out of the time freeze.

"The time freeze won't last much longer, but however long it does, it'll be longer than the time it takes for my patience to run out."

"You... you're insane."

"No, I'm just angry." Patsy was raising her arm, ready to reach into his chest.

The words spilled out of the bass player's mouth in rapid succession. "She's at the Art Gallery. The director... she had a secret apartment created for her. She has the book on display in her office." An uneasy pause followed, filled only by the terrified man hyperventilating. "Can I go now?"

"If I ever feel your presence in this world again, so help me..."

"I get the picture."

A ghostly shadow came out of the bass player and disappeared, leaving the freed bass player locked in the time freeze. Glenda stood behind Jai and grabbed his shoulders as she addressed Patsy. "I don't want you going anywhere near my son ever again."

Jai looked over his shoulder. "Huh?"

Patsy's jaw dropped. "What?"

"You heard me. I want you to stay away from my son."

"But... I just got rid of three mind thieves and found out where your daughter is—"

"You were cruel."

"But they were Nasqa."

"Cruelty is still cruelty, no matter who it's perpetrated against."

Her jaw hanging open, Patsy glanced at Jai. He shrugged his shoulders and said, "I kinda agree with Mum on the cruelty bit."

"But... they're Nasqa... mind thieves. They are the great nuisance of the Crossworlds."

Glenda replied, "Does that justify tearing them into pieces like that? Do you take joy in telling them they face an eternity of pain and suffering?"

Feeling weakness in her knees, Patsy stumbled to a nearby chair and sat down. "But your daughter—"

"But this, but that—for someone with such a big reputation, you're pretty damn good at making excuses. Of course I want my daughter back, but not at any cost. You can measure a person's worth by how they treat their foes."

Patsy leaned forward, her head almost dangling between her knees. Her voice was barely audible. "You shouldn't use magic the way you do."

Glenda's fingernails dug into Jai's shoulder as her muscles tightened. Her breaths were coming in short gasps and her teeth were clenched. "Excuse me?"

Patsy raised her head a little, just enough to make eye contact. "The magic you use on stage, it has consequences—"

"Don't give me that mumbo-jumbo. You're as bad as my mother." She released her grip on Jai's shoulder and grabbed her bag from a nearby table. "Come on, Jai, we're leaving. I've had enough of this."

Jai took a step back from her. "No!"

"What do you mean, no?" She glared at Patsy. "What have you done to my son?"

Jai stood with his arms straight by his side and his fists clenched. "I mean no."

"Well, that's just great, isn't it? I thought you were with me on this. For fifteen years I thought I'd lost you. Just when I thought I'd got you back, it turns out that I've lost you anyway."

"It's not like that. I'm sorry it's taken so long. It must have hurt real bad. But I'm not going to walk out that door with you now."

Glenda stood with her mouth open and a hand against her chest. "My poor baby! What has she done to you?"

"You can drop the act, Mum. I agree with you about what she did to the Nasqa, but we've still got to try and get Mel back."

Glenda slipped the bag off her shoulder and slammed it down on the table. "Ugh! You saw what the little monster just did here. Can you imagine what else she's capable of?"

Glenda spun around at the sound of Patsy's voice. "Not as much as what we're capable of if we work together."

"Come again?"

Patsy stood up. "We can form a Trinity that the Nasqa will fear so much they'll likely flee this world without us having to even threaten them."

"Oh really, just like that? And how do you propose we form this Trinity? We're kind of short one generation of witches."

Jai said, "I've been in a Trinity of Power with her before. And she's right. The Nasqa will fear us if we work together."

"You've done what?" she looked at Patsy. "Is there no end to your madness?"

"She saved my life, Mum. We wouldn't be here talking now if not for her courage and determination."

"You did see what I saw?"

"Yes, but trust me, she really is our best hope."

"They're going to be waiting for you." The three of them turned around to see the drummer addressing them. The time freeze had lifted.

The bass player was struggling to get to his feet. "Oh man, these clothes stink." He looked at Patsy and said, "I'd love to stick around and thank you, but I've got to get home and have a shower… and a change of clothes."

Glenda asked, "You are aware of what she did to that thing?"

"Oh yeah. And I'll be forever in her debt."

"What she did was cruel."

"Oh yeah? Let me tell you, Glenda, you don't know what cruelty is until you have one of those things controlling you."

The lead guitarist strode across and pushed against the drummer's shoulder. "Is that so? Maybe you shouldn't have resisted, you little wuss."

The bass player turned back from making his way to the door and wedged himself between them, pushing against the guitarist. "Hey, go easy. What's your beef?"

"The Crimson Dockers never would've been a hit without our little friends driving us. Do you really think any of us can play like that without them?" He turned and pointed an accusing finger at Patsy. "And it's all your fault."

Patsy's voice was deadpan. "Of course you can. You just have to believe in yourself. It was your hands doing the playing."

The band manager, an old hippie with long grey hair tied back in a ponytail, came across. "Hey, is there a problem here?" He looked over his shoulder to the crowd of party guests staring at the band members. "There's a whole lot of people hanging out to meet you guys."

The guitarist replied, "I was just in the process of telling Glenda and the boys that I quit."

"What are you talking about?"

The guitarist looked across at Jai and Glenda, then turned his attention to Patsy as he sneered, "Let's just put it down to family issues." He turned and took long strides as he departed, turning to flick the room the bird as he walked out the door.

The manager stood staring at the now empty doorway as if he might somehow be able to will the musician back.

"It's okay, Rick, let him go." Glenda put her bag back over her shoulder. "I've got a few family issues of my own that I need to deal with." She glared at Patsy. "Are you coming or what?" As the three of them left the party Glenda muttered under her breath, "This really goes against my better judgement, but it seems I don't have much choice."

*

Kellie Mercier, director of the Art Gallery of New South Wales, strolled through the door leading to the secret apartment. Her simple alpaca wool dress clung to her slender figure. "Hello, my dear."

Mel was slumped in a luxurious leather couch. She looked up from her book and replied, "Hello, Mother."

Kellie ran a hand through her silver, shoulder-length hair. "I've just learned we're likely to have some visitors shortly."

A smile erupted across Mel's face. "Really? It's been so long since we've had visitors! Is it Uncle Ben and Aunty Jan?" She put her book aside. "Uncle Ben always brings me new books to read. And I do so enjoy Aunty Jan's stories about going to the moon when she was in Buzz Aldrin's body."

Kellie smiled as she watched Mel's enthusiasm.

Mel noticed a tear running down Kellie's cheek. "What's wrong, Mother?"

Kellie sighed. "I so wish I could say it was our kin who are coming."

"Who is it then?"

"It's your birth mother. She's with her son."

Mel's eyes lit up. "I get to see my brother?"

"Darling, this is serious. They want to take you away from me."

"But why would they want to do that?"

"They're being influenced by someone else. A ghost from the past. Someone so evil the very thought of her sends a shiver up my spine. She's caused more harm to the Nasqa than anyone else in history. She's obsessed with keeping us from helping humanity reach its fullest potential."

Mel's expression conveyed her lack of understanding. "Who is this ghost? Why would anyone want to interfere with the Nasqa's benevolence?"

Kellie took a seat next to her on the couch. "Well, 'ghost' probably isn't the best term. One of your ancestors has travelled through time, with the sole aim of trying to take you away from me."

"Why would anyone want to do that? I'm happy here with you."

"I know you are." She placed a hand on Mel's knee. "But there are those who are motivated by greed and a lust for power. That's why I've had to be so careful about protecting you from the rest of the world."

"Protecting me? Sometimes I wonder why that's even necessary."

"Have I not given you everything you've ever wanted? Would I do for a prisoner the things I do for you? Yes, I'm protecting you, from monsters like the one who's on her way here now."

Mel cast her eyes downward. "Mother, I do love being here with you. But I wonder sometimes, when will I be able to leave the gallery building? I want to walk through the city with everyone else."

"Melanie." Kellie's voice took on a more serious tone. "We've been through this a thousand times. Do we really have to go over it again? You know I don't like having to repeat myself."

Mel shook her head then started to cry.

Kellie stood up and threw her arms into the air. "For fifteen years I've been trying to tell you. Read the book with me and I'll be able to fully protect you. Then, and only then, will it be safe for you to go out into the city."

"But you know what happens when I try to read it. It's like it gets angry with me and pushes me away."

"Melanie! You're twenty-three years old. You're not a little girl anymore. How on Earth do you expect the Nasqa to help humanity find a better future if you're not prepared to conquer your fears?"

"Why don't you just read it yourself then?"

"You know that's not possible."

"Why?"

"I'm trying to protect you."

"That's not an answer."

"Don't you want to protect me too?"

"How am I meant to do that?"

"If we go into my office now and we read the book together, we can stop your birth mother from taking you away." There was a long pause. "Do you remember the last time we read it together… when you were fourteen?"

Mel nodded.

"Do you remember what we did afterwards?"

"We went for a walk in the Botanic Gardens."

"And wasn't that a lovely day?"

Mel looked up at Kellie. "But the dreams I had after that… the ones with the wood-elf. He told me that I shouldn't read it with you."

Kellie sat next to her again and put an arm around her shoulders. "Oh, my poor baby. They were just dreams. And you do remember what I've told you about wood-elves, I hope?"

Mel nodded. "They can't be trusted."

"That's right." Kellie gave Mel a big hug. "As long as you trust in me, I promise I'll keep you safe. But for me to be able to fulfill that promise, we need to read the book together. And we need to read it now." Kellie relaxed her hold on Mel then looked into her eyes and smiled. "You know what? If we can use the book to get rid of your birth mother, and make sure that she never comes back, I think it might just be safe enough for you to go out into the city."

Mel's eyes widened. "Really?"

Kellie's grin grew as she nodded. "Yes! You'd be able to go wherever you want."

Mel threw her arms around Kellie. "Oh, thank you, Mother." After a long hug she stood up and declared, "Okay, I'll do it. Let's go to your office and do some reading."

•

"I'm sorry about your band." Patsy was right behind Glenda and Jai.

"Oh yeah? You could've fooled me." Glenda refused to look over her shoulder as she addressed Patsy while they walked down the corridor toward her dressing room.

"Don't worry, she'll get over it." Jai's voice was almost a whisper.

"Are you sure about that?" replied Patsy.

Glenda came to a dead stop just outside the dressing room door and spun around. "What did I tell you about staying away from my son? Just because I'm willing to give this Trinity thing of yours a shot, doesn't mean I'm happy for you to talk to him."

Jai asked, "Don't you think that's being a little unrealistic?"

Glenda's sharp glare switched its hold from Patsy to her son. "I think everything about this girl is unrealistic, especially her reputation for performing good deeds."

"Whatever you may think of me, Jai's still right." Patsy took a deep breath. *Stay calm. Getting angry isn't going to help.* "If we want the Trinity to work, we need to be thinking in harmony with each other."

"Well, that's just great, isn't it? How's this going to work anyway? I thought it was supposed to be three consecutive generations of women to make a Trinity work."

"That's ideal, but not necessary. As long as we're all the same bloodline, we can make it work."

"I think you're just making this up."

Patsy closed her eyes. *This is her problem, don't let it be yours.*

"Mum, haven't you listened to anything either of us has said? I told you, I've already been in a Trinity with her. That's how we escaped."

"How do you know it was a real Trinity and not just her telling you that's what it was? You never used to talk to me like that. What's she done to you?"

"I'm not a little kid anymore, Mum!"

"Oh, really? All of fifteen years old and all grown up, huh? You have no idea what I've been through for you."

"How about what I've been through for you?"

"Excuse me! Ever tried giving birth? Have you been through that for me?"

"How appropriate. You decide to talk about giving birth while you're treating me like a baby."

"You are a baby. You're my baby."

"I wish I'd stayed in Patsy's time. Her family were—"

"Stop it!" Patsy clenched her fists and stamped a foot for emphasis. The resulting shockwave shook the building and sent Glenda and Jai to the floor. Glenda's head hit hard against the door frame of her dressing room.

Seeing his mother slumped in the doorway, Jai lurched across and cupped his hand under the back of her head. "Are you alright, Mum?" Glenda's hair felt warm, wet, and sticky. There was blood, and lots of it. A small puddle was forming on the floor.

Glenda groaned, "Yes, I'll be okay."

"Is anyone hurt?" The three of them turned around to see a security guard at the end of the corridor. He started running toward them when he noticed the dark red pool of blood in the doorway.

Glenda looked at Patsy and said, "Okay, you made your point. If we're going to do this, we'll need to go now, otherwise we'll just end up spending the night waiting for stitches at the hospital."

Patsy pushed a hand toward the guard causing him to appear as though running in extreme slow motion.

Glenda's jaw dropped. "How did you do that?"

"The three of us being together makes all our powers stronger."

"All of us?" Glenda looked at Jai then back to Patsy. "Last I knew, Jai didn't have any powers."

"When Patsy saved my life, she had to share some of her powers with me."

Glenda shook her head. "I'm scared of what the devil in the detail is to this story." She glanced at the guard still inching toward them. "Let's just get this over with."

Patsy wrapped her arms around them, closed her eyes, and said, "Imagine we're at the Art Gallery."

The guard came to a stop at the empty door, puzzled by how the trio had disappeared. This was the second time tonight he'd imagined seeing people who turned out to not be there. But the pool of blood was real. He looked inside the empty dressing room then squatted to inspect the scarlet evidence of Glenda's injury.

*

"I don't understand." Patsy was looking at the contemporary works filling the walls around them. "Weren't we supposed to be going to an art gallery?"

Glenda stood up and approached a large canvas with a heavily textured splash of black paint going from one corner to another. "Invigorating, isn't it?"

"Shh!" said Jai. "There's bound to be security guards."

Glenda shook her head, "No, it's all electronic these days, all driven by AI." She pointed to the myriad of small, dark domes attached to the ceiling. "See all those cameras? They'll have detected us and notified the police by now. So, I guess we'd better be quick."

"We can put the building in a time freeze if we need to," said Patsy.

"We? Don't you mean you?" replied Glenda.

Patsy looked around at the size of the building with its cavernous halls disappearing in every direction and metal staircases leading to levels above and below where they stood. "It's too big for me to do on my own straight after allowing us to be here. We'd need to do it together."

Glenda's expression made her cynicism obvious. "Maybe we should just forget that for now and focus on things we're all a bit more familiar with."

Patsy's bewildered expression made it clear these surroundings were anything but familiar to her.

Jai headed toward the static escalators. "Shouldn't we be heading down to the basement if time's an issue?"

"Yes," replied Glenda. She looked at Patsy. "Come on, we can't waste time spacing out on the art."

"But they're not in the basement. I can tell. They're with the Book of Wisdom."

"And you know this because?"

"I've written in the Book of Wisdom, I'm attached to it." Patsy continued staring into space. "And I've written so much more in it now than I had in my time… I feel like I'm part of it, like I can see everything around it."

Glenda's expression changed. She could tell that Patsy was telling the truth.

"There's two women. They've opened the book. One is older with straight silver hair that's down to her shoulders. The other one is younger. She has long, wavy, red hair and freckles."

Glenda gasped. "Melanie!"

"The older woman can't make out the words in the book, but the younger one can. She's reading it out to her… she's reading the Book of Wisdom to a Nasqa!" Patsy looked around at Glenda and Jai. "We have to stop her."

"Well, that is kinda why we're here," replied Glenda.

"Do you know where they are?" asked Jai.

"I don't need to. Take my hands. I can take us to where the book is."

.

Melanie gasped and stepped back, her hand grabbing at her chest when the Book of Wisdom slammed shut.

"What was that?" asked Kellie.

She turned when a voice from behind her spoke out. "It was me."

Kellie and Mel glared at Patsy. She looked somehow more powerful as she stood in her torn jeans and t-shirt than Kellie had expected. Her steely gaze spoke of a confidence beyond her years. Hands on hips, she was flanked by Glenda and Jai. Kellie took a step toward the trio, ensuring that she placed herself between them and Mel. "Well, well, well. I'd been told you three might by dropping by." She tapped a finger against her chin while she looked Patsy up and down. "I'm not sure if I prefer your quaint nineteenth-century attire or your new look. They're both rather dull, I must say."

"What are you talking about?" Patsy's expression betrayed a hairline crack in her confidence. She tried to cover for it by sneering as she followed up. "I don't know you."

"Ah, yes, but I know you." Kellie was grinning as she waved a finger in the air for emphasis. "You were always quite a thorn in my side. Back in the day, when I inhabited Governor Pritchard's body, you caused all manner of problems for me and my men as we tried to maintain order. Every time I hatched a plan to get my hands on the book, there was Patricia McIntyre, always getting in the way."

"And now I'm here to get it back."

Kellie put her hands up in mock fear. "Oh no, the cranky little witch has come to take her book away."

"You can keep the damn book." Glenda stepped forward and continued. "I'm just here to take my daughter back."

"No!" Patsy snapped.

"My, we are a united team, aren't we? The aging, wounded hippie who relies on misusing magic to make a living, her hapless adolescent son, and a cranky little girl who's nowhere near the height of her powers." She turned back to Glenda. "Oh, and please, do try not to bleed too much on the carpet. It's awfully difficult to get out, you know."

Mel looked at Glenda. "Why are you doing this? Why would I want to go with you?"

"I'm your mother."

"Then why didn't you act like one? This is where I belong"—she stepped up to Kellie and took her hand—"with my real mother."

A tear rolled down Glenda's cheek. "But I…" Her jaw hung open, but she couldn't find any words.

Kellie grinned. "See? You really are wasting your time." She put an arm around Mel. "How about you three toddle off now and stop upsetting my daughter?" She blew Glenda a kiss. "Nice of you to drop by."

Glenda's expression went blank as she lowered her hand and started drawing energy from the Crossworlds. She whispered, "I'm not leaving without my daughter." Her breaths were growing short and sharp.

Kellie snickered then turned her attention to Jai as he stepped forward to address his sister. "Mel, do you remember me?"

Mel choked back a tear as she looked at him. "Yes, of course I do." She pulled away from Kellie and took a step toward him. A nervous giggle escaped as she said, "It's funny, you seemed so much bigger in my memories."

"Well, hey, you were only eight, so that's to be expected." He took a step closer. "I've risked my life travelling through time trying to find you, and well, I'm kinda sorry that it's taken me fifteen years to get here." He reached out to her. "Please, Mel, let's go home and make up for those years we lost." He glared at Kellie. "Years we lost because of what she's done to you."

"What's she's done to me?"

"Can't you see? She's turned you against us."

"How can you say that?" Mel turned to Kellie for reassurance then looked back to Jai. "She's been kinder than your mother ever was. I feel loved. I never knew how that felt before Mother rescued me."

"Then do it for us, for you and me."

"I can't, and I don't want to. Can't you see? I could never do that to her, not after what she's done for me."

"She's Nasqa, a mind thief. She takes over people's lives, and when one life wears out, she takes another."

"No, you're wrong to judge her like that. The Nasqa are doing everything they can to make the world a place that's safe for humanity. The human race is forever staging wars, trying to tear one another down. That doesn't help us, and it doesn't help the Nasqa. They benefit from humanity being stable and happy as much as we do."

Patsy sneered. "The Nasqa just want to enslave people, nothing more, nothing less."

Mel shook her head. "No, they're not like that." She looked at Kellie. "Mother is the kindest person I know."

That was enough for Glenda. "In that case, I need to get you out to meet a few more people." She lurched forward and hurled a ball of energy at Kellie, only to find herself flying backwards.

Kellie laughed. "You really should be more careful, what with that nasty wound and all."

Patsy also threw her hand forward, only to find that she too was flung backwards as the energy rebounded off Kellie and went straight back to her.

Kellie walked up to Patsy and stood over her stunned face. "Melanie and I found a wonderful little spell to protect us from magic that comes from anyone in her own bloodline. Let's see now…" She smiled before continuing. "That would equal all of you." She leaned over so her face was near Patsy's. "Oh, and that little trick you learned from your friend Kerridwen… the one about reaching in to grab me out of this body? You'll be in a whole world of pain if you try that one."

The sound of approaching sirens caused Kellie to look over her shoulder to the window. "That'll be the police on their way to lock you up for breaking into the gallery." She turned to Mel. "Your brother's still standing there like a stunned mullet. Perhaps you should do something about that, before he gets any heroic ideas?"

Mel shook her head. "But… I can't, Mother. He's my brother."

"Melanie, you know I wouldn't ask you to do this if it wasn't absolutely necessary. You need to show him your power, or he's liable to do something stupid."

"What, like this?" Jai charged at Kellie and lunged. Seeing Kellie threatened forced Mel to act. She extended her hand toward Jai. He became airborne, hitting his head hard as he landed. The impact left him unconscious.

Mel ran up and crouched next to his slumped form. "Oh, why did you have to go and threaten Mother like that?"

Kellie looked at Patsy and Glenda. "Either of you two want to have another try?" She approached Patsy, who was still winded from the impact of her attempt at bringing down her tormentor. "What's the matter, Witch? Cat got your tongue?"

Patsy wasn't paying attention. She was focused on Mel. With Jai unconscious, the Trinity was broken. But a new one existed. With three generations of women from the same bloodline present, the Trinity was like a magnetic force drawing the three together. Patsy opened her mind to Mel's, revealing all she knew about the Nasqa. *Reach out to your mother, learn the truth.* Mel turned to Glenda.

Kellie gave Patsy a short kick in the stomach. "Hey, I'm talking to you."

Patsy spluttered up some blood, then smiled. "You're making a big mistake."

Two police officers accompanied by the representative of the gallery's security firm entered the director's office. "What seems to be the problem here?"

Patsy gestured toward the three of them and locked them in a time freeze.

"Really?" Kellie looked at the frozen officers then turned her attention back to Patsy, bringing her foot back in preparation for another kick. "You are just so annoying."

"I wouldn't do that if I were you." Glenda had got to her feet and was reaching into the Crossworlds to draw power for another strike at Kellie.

"You don't learn, do you?" Kellie looked at Mel. "Could you please do something about that birth mother of yours?" Mel drew her arm back to draw power herself. Glenda swung her arm, this time letting a cord of energy come forth from her hand, almost like she was swinging a rope. It pulled a nearby marble bust from its plinth, sending it hurtling toward Kellie, not caring that Patsy was also in its path. Mel threw her arm forward in response. The bust shattered, its pieces flying back toward Glenda. A large piece struck her on the head, causing her to fall to the ground, blood gushing from a fresh wound above her right eye.

Kellie turned her attention back to Patsy. "Try holding a time freeze after this." She put as much energy as she could into swinging her foot.

"No, Mother, wait!"

Kellie's foot stopped just short of making contact with Patsy again. She turned to Mel.

"We should let the police deal with them."

"Why?"

"Because we're better than them. You're better than them."

"If we want the police to help, we need to knock her out of action to break the time freeze."

Mel thought of all the images Patsy and Glenda had filled her head with. Nasqa being ripped from bodies by pixies, by Kerridwen, and by Patsy. Nasqa torn apart and hurled into the void. Nasqa treated like vermin. She joined her mother standing over her. "Please Mother, let me look after this." She drew her arm up then slammed a ball of energy into Patsy's head.

.

Patsy's head hurt. She had no idea where she was. To make it worse, the constant, high-pitched 'bing' that she heard every few seconds was annoying beyond belief. She tried opening her eyes, but the bright light made the pain in her head worse. When she closed her eyes again, it felt like the room was spinning, making her want to vomit.

Bing!… Bing!… Bing!

Then she felt the thing in her arm. She grabbed hold of it, then a hand grabbed hold of hers. "Whoa, whoa, whoa. Slow down, Pats."

She forced herself to open her eyes at the sound of Jai's voice. "Where am I?"

"Royal Prince Alfred Hospital. You've been out for most of the day."

"What's this thing in my arm?"

"It's called an IV drip." Jai pointed to the plastic bag hovering above Patsy's head. "It's like a kind of food that gets fed straight into your blood."

"Then, why am I so hungry?"

Jai laughed. "Don't worry, now that you're awake, you'll be able to eat something soon." He looked over his shoulder to the door. "Right after the police have finished questioning you."

"Urgh! Let's just get out of here. We've still got to get your sister back."

Jai went silent.

Bing!... Bing!... Bing!

"What is that noise?"

"It's monitoring your pulse."

"Why?"

"Patsy, you almost died. My sister, she hit you hard. The doctors say you've got a really bad concussion."

The memory of the look in Mel's eyes as she threw her arm toward Patsy swamped through her head, causing it to spin once more. Seeing Patsy's eyes roll up into her head, Jai grabbed hold of her, wrapping his arms around her shoulders. "Hey, it's going to be okay." Again, he looked over his shoulder, then back to Patsy. "You've got no choice. When the police come in, you'll have to answer their questions. Mum's told them you're my cousin, Jess. That your Mum's name is Paula, and you came down with me to watch Mum's band."

Before Patsy had a chance to reply, the door opened and two police officers walked through, a man who was taller than anyone Patsy had ever met and a woman whose face lit up as she approached the bed. "Hey you, welcome back to the land of the living."

The tall officer looked at Jai "Shouldn't you be checking on your Mum?"

Jai nodded and started towards the door. "I'll see you soon, Jess."

•

"So, what else did they ask you?" Glenda cast a glance at Patsy via the rearview mirror as they sped along the freeway on their way back to the Blue Mountains.

"I don't remember."

"What do you mean, 'you don't remember'?"

"Go easy on her Mum, she's got a concussion."

Glenda looked across at her son in the passenger seat. "Yeah, and I've got a dozen stitches in my head. Despite everything, I still stuck my neck out for her and lied to the cops on her behalf, so I figure the least she could do is give a few honest answers."

"Really, I can't remember," Patsy protested.

"Yeah, you said that before. Perhaps you can try harder."

"They kept asking me questions that I didn't know how to answer."

Glenda looked at the road ahead and nodded before responding. "Well, there you go. The girl who had all the answers when she arrived, declaring she was going to save us all, is suddenly lost for words."

Silence.

"Did you tell them about how you broke up my band?"

More silence.

"Or, how you destroyed any chance of me getting my daughter back?"

"Mum, don't you think you've made your point already?"

"No, I don't. How do you sum up fifteen years of planning to get your baby back being flushed down the toilet by a teenager's arrogance in twenty questions? Do you have an answer for that? I've got no choice but to ferry her back to my home just to be rid of her. So, please excuse me for wanting to get a few answers on the way."

Patsy whispered, "I'm sorry."

Silence.

•

Patsy and Jai walked down the steps toward the pool. "I'll come back soon and we'll try again."

"No, Patsy, it's not worth it. Mum's never going to trust you, ever."

"I know that. But you still trust me, don't you? And Nan, she still talks to me."

Jai let out a sigh. "You saved my life and risked your own doing it. I'll always be grateful for that. But that was in a different world, one where we were both out of place. This is my world, and somehow, your moral judgements don't work as well here as they did when we were facing blow darts and wrathapillars."

"I'm sorry."

"Yeah, so am I."

Patsy felt a hammer banging in her head that reminded her of the noise from the machine in the hospital.

As she approached the water's edge, she found herself focusing on the need to get back home so she could release the people she loved most in the world from the void. She longed for her family, for Cook's food, and Clara's conversation. She longed for the reassurance of her father's moral authority and strength.

She wanted to go home and lick her wounds.

Jai grabbed her shoulder. "Hey, snap out of it, Pats. You can't wander into the pool without saying goodbye. This is the last time we'll ever see each other."

"It doesn't have to be."

"Umm, you might want to talk to my mum about that. Actually, on second thoughts, that's probably not a good idea."

The water in the pool was stirring, beckoning Patsy to return to where she belonged.

She started walking into the water. What would her family make of her new clothing? How would she face telling them about her failure? Most important of all, would Glenda and Jai be able to strike up a new plan to get Mel back?

"It's not your fault." It was as though Jai was reading her mind. "You risked your life to try. And hey, that Nasqa had done a real job on Mel. I don't know that any plan would've worked."

A hint of a smile appeared on Patsy's otherwise dour expression.

"Hey!" Jai followed her into the water. He handed Patsy his phone. "Take this, that way I can message you and let you know when we succeed in getting Mel back. As long as the phone is near the portal, it should work."

"But don't you need it?"

"I need a new one anyway... Take this one, and we can keep in touch."

"Won't that upset your mother?"

"She doesn't have to know."

"Goodbye and thank you... thank you for everything." Patsy turned away and walked into the vortex.

"See you, Pats. Take care of yourself."

*

"It's about time." Neridah's frustration was obvious as she berated her granddaughter.

"Aye, it feels as though we've been trapped in here for an eternity." The Reverend's gaze carried an unspoken accusation.

Meredith's tone was softer. "I'm just glad you made it back safely."

The water swirled around Patsy as she approached the shore,

clutching Jai's phone to her chest. "I'm sorry, I didn't feel like I had a choice." She looked up, preparing to continue, but the three images grew more distant and were breaking apart. Patsy's heart raced as she reached out to try and grab hold of them. "I'm going to get you out of there... I promise!" *Surely they'll be okay. It's only because I'm coming out of the portal that they've disappeared... surely.*

The wind was howling as she emerged from the pool. The trees had all been stripped of their leaves and a gritty dust made it difficult to see far ahead. She reached the shore, then turned around and saw the wind had swept all the water from the pool outside of the vortex itself. Trees had fallen across the sandstone steps that led up to the paddock. She held one arm up to shield her eyes from the dust as she fought against the wind and struggled to get up the stairs. Her mother, Nana-Neri, and the Reverend would just have to wait a bit longer. To try and rescue them in this storm would be unthinkable.

As she worked her way through the paddock toward the house, the dust-filled wind tore at Patsy's flesh and clothing. She put the phone in her back pocket and tucked her t-shirt into her jeans to try and keep it from blowing up like a loose-fitting dress on a windy day.

On nearing the house, she saw that nothing remained of the stables other than their framework. The front door and most of the window shutters had been stripped from the house. She watched in horror as parts of the veranda were torn away, disintegrating into dust as they hurtled through the air.

Falling in through the front door brought some respite from the gale. She yelled as loud as she could to try to be heard above the wind's deafening howl. "Father!" There was no answer. "Cook! Father! Is there anyone here?" She thought for a moment that she could hear someone crying in one of the rooms. She made her way along the corridor, then opened the imposing door to the library. Inside, she found Clara Jenkins huddled in the corner holding Ferdinand.

She ran across to her tutor. "Miss Jenkins, what's going on? Where's Father?"

Clara struggled to get the words out through her tears. "Your father... I'm so sorry... he's... he was taken away by Captain Taylor. He... he's dead."

The words didn't register, didn't seem real. "What about Cook, where's Cook?"

Clara sat shaking her head. She looked down at the cat she was rocking back and forth.

"Where's Cook?"

"I watched it happen."

"Watched what happen?"

"The storm. It took Cook. It took everyone."

"Miss Jenkins, you're not making sense."

"I saw it with my own eyes."

"What did you see?"

"The dust... this storm... it's not of this world."

Clara released the cat, then threw her arms around Patsy, crying into her shoulder. Patsy returned the hug and watched as Ferdinand ran out the door, disintegrating into dust and drifting away on the wind as he went. Patsy struggled to comprehend what she'd just seen. "Did Cook do that? Turn into dust... then blow away in the wind?"

There was no answer. Patsy hugged her tutor tighter, feeling a desperate need for her familiar warmth and reassurance. Instead, Clara disintegrated in Patsy's arms. Clothing, flesh, hair, all turned to dust and blew away.

Patsy looked around at what was left in the room. The Book of

Wisdom was on its stand. Her only hope would lie within its pages, of that, she was sure. But she'd have to take it somewhere safe. She tried a time-freeze, but it was ineffective.

Krinkle-myst's cabin! Being outside the known universe, that was bound to be safe. She grabbed the book and allowed herself to be at the bottom of the paddock near the portal that led to the land that no one's ever seen.

CHAPTER 7

Patsy plummeted then slammed into the ground near the bottom of the paddock. She found herself a few paces away from the wood-elf. Krinkle-myst watched Patsy struggle to lift herself from the ground. It appeared the wind had little effect on him.

The Book of Wisdom landed with a thud between them. Patsy called out to the wood-elf, but her words disappeared into the wind.

She rose to her knees, then looked into the wood-elf's eyes, his stature being such that, even on her knees, she was still almost twice his height. "I need to get them back."

The wood-elf gestured toward the book. "You won't find the answer in there."

"That can't be. It must be in there somewhere. I need to take the book to your cabin so I can find the answer."

"The land that no one's ever seen won't let you in, not until you repair the damage you and your friend have done to the fabric holding the timelines together."

"But how can I do that without the book to guide me? I can't even form a Trinity of Power. Everyone's gone."

"And there won't ever be another Trinity unless you can repair the damage. Thanks to your reckless actions, history is now being wiped away from countless millions of timelines. If you don't act soon, all timelines within this range of crossworlds will be gone, and all that will be left of it is you. You and an empty universe."

Dust combined with Patsy's tears to create brown streaks on her cheeks. "I can't do anything right."

"Feeling sorry for yourself won't help anyone."

"I just make everything worse."

"Well, it's about time you look at turning that trend around."

"I don't know how."

"You'd better come up with something… and sooner rather than later."

She looked around. There was no sign of the house now at the top of the hill, and all the trees were gone. She had no way of knowing where she was. "How can I undo any of this? I don't even know where to start."

"You can start by going back to Jai's timeline, to the moment before the foolish boy decided to play the hero, and you can stop him."

"That's easy for you to say. I don't even know how to find my way to the right timeline."

"Do I really have to spell everything out for you?"

Patsy started sobbing. "I'll just make things worse if I try to fix it."

Krinkle-myst looked around, then turned back to Patsy. "I have to say, making things worse than they already are would be quite a feat."

Patsy nodded, wiping her eyes dry. "Okay, I'll try. But please, you must have some idea of how I can get there."

"You've carved out a deep trail. It's like when you walk through long grass. The more you walk a certain path, the more pronounced it becomes." He pointed to her back pocket. "And his phone will help guide you. It feels compelled to return to its own time. You can force it with your will to guide you so that you arrive a few minutes earlier than when he left to come here."

"Then what?"

"Stop him."

"How?"

"You'll work it out."

"And after that?"

"Then, the timelines will be restored to what they were, and no one but you will remember what happened."

"What about you?"

"I think I'd rather forget. But my burden is that I always end up remembering these things." Krinkle-myst removed his glasses and rubbed at his right eye. "Now, I'm going back to the land that no one's ever seen so Mrs Krinkle-myst can help me get a speck of dust out of my eye."

"Wait! Before you go… how am I going to find the portal when everything's already turned to dust?"

"You're really not very good at listening, are you?"

"But—" Patsy found herself talking to the wind. The wood-elf was gone.

Now, with the timelines progressively turning to dust, she felt more alone than ever before.

You're really not good at listening…

Listening to what?

Patsy tried to shut out the sound of the wind and reflected on what Krinkle-myst might have been talking about. What had he discussed with her recently? What was new to her in what he'd been saying? She thought back to when she and Jai had been to see him and he'd tried to explain about the timelines, about future and past memories. What she needed was somewhere in what he'd had to say about the timelines.

Sometimes, just being sad enough about an event in your past will actually shift you into a version of reality where whatever it was that happened was worse than it really was.

The parallel timelines. The way he'd spoken about them suggested they were almost countless in number. And, if it was possible to slip between them, maybe Patsy could communicate with versions of herself in different timelines. Maybe she could find one where the portal hadn't yet turned to dust. Maybe that other version of herself could guide her to the portal... despite everything of substance in this one having turned to dust. She thought of what she'd learned from the Seer when going inside Jai, how she'd gone deep within herself to help him. She'd felt the connection then, the connection to versions of herself in other timelines.

The tears stopped and Patsy's sadness was flushed away by grim determination.

She could do this.

She had to.

.

Patsy closed her eyes and allowed herself to accept the sound of the wind for what it was.

She allowed herself to accept the pain of her loss.

She allowed herself to accept the guilt.

Most of all, she allowed herself to be at peace with herself as she sought guidance to the portal. Millions of Patsy McIntyres were experiencing the destruction of their universe, but only one had any understanding as to why it was happening. And those Patsy McIntyres who were lost in confusion about what was happening were drawn to this one who knew. They were drawn to her pleading for guidance. Most important of all, there were those who lived in worlds where the portal hadn't yet been wiped away, not many, but enough.

With her eyes closed, she started walking. She could feel a picture around her coming into focus of how the property was before the dust, how it still existed in some worlds.

She walked further, becoming more confident with each step.

Then, as she neared the pathway leading down to the pool that housed the portal, the image started to fade. The pathway leading to the pool was vanishing from the parallel universes at an increasing pace. But she was getting close now, close enough that she could feel the power of the portal. She held Jai's phone and felt it pulling her toward the portal.

She had to be careful with the placement of her feet. There were no carved steps anymore, just a steep slope of dust.

The vision that had guided her was completely gone by the time the sloping dust had levelled out, indicating to her she had reached the location of the portal. She kept her eyes closed as she walked into the centre of where the pool would have been and became conscious of a shift in how the dust was moving. It was swirling around her.

She knew she was successful when she opened her eyes and saw water instead of dust. She'd arrived in Jai's timeline.

*

Glenda embraced her son. "Don't forget to call me when you get there. As long as you're near the portal, the phone should work."

"Don't worry, Mum." Jai pulled away from her and walked toward the pool.

"And remember, you'll need to call me when you're ready to come back so I can open the portal."

"Yeah, I got that the first ten thousand times you told me." He looked back over his shoulder. "Are you going to open it up or what?"

Glenda's expression went blank. She stared past her son toward the pool. "It looks like I don't need to."

Jai turned back toward the pool to see the water in the middle was swirling. The centre shallowed to reveal an adolescent girl in torn jeans and a tattered Stevie Nicks t-shirt. Her long hair was matted and she was covered in dirt and scratches. Her face reminded him of photos he'd seen of his grandmother as a young girl. Could it be?

Glenda and Jai approached the edge of the pool as Patsy made her way toward the shore. Glenda's voice trembled as she asked, "Who are you, and what do you want?"

A tear welled up in Patsy's eye as she looked at Glenda and saw Nana-Neri in every feature… Nana-Neri who'd turned to dust while trapped in the void. Could she stop that happening?

"Hello, I'm waiting. Who are you and what do you want?"

She even sounds like Nana-Neri. Patsy looked at Jai and thought of how much younger he looked now than the boy she'd shared so much with as they'd laid the groundwork for the destruction of everything. *All that we went through… and for what?* She took a deep breath to compose herself. "I'm Patricia, Patricia McIntyre. I've come to stop you from making a big mistake, the biggest mistake anyone could ever make."

"I didn't know they wore jeans and t-shirts in the nineteenth century."

Patsy looked at Glenda. "Your mother bought me these fifteen years from now."

"I don't believe you." Glenda positioned herself to be standing between Patsy and her son. "Your timing seems like a coincidence too extreme to be possible. Tell me the truth. Who are you, and how could you know what we have planned?"

As Patsy continued moving toward them, Glenda and Jai were stepping back. Glenda was lowering her hand to draw power from the Crossworlds. Patsy pleaded with her. "What you're about to do, it's a terrible mistake."

"Stop right there."

"The consequences..." Patsy looked to the ground, choking back tears. "Everything will be lost."

"It can't be as bad as the consequences of not going," said Jai. "I need to find my sister."

Glenda turned to her son. "What did I tell you about not telling anyone about this?"

"I swear, Mum, I never breathed a word to anyone before now." Jai gestured toward Patsy. "What if she really is who she says she is?"

"More likely the Nasqa have found out what we're doing." She addressed Patsy. "You might as well leave her body now. We're not fooled." She turned back to Jai. "I'm going to open the portal, are you ready?"

"You can't! You can't do it! I can't let you!" Patsy collapsed on the shore as the water settled behind her. She was still clutching the phone. She buried her face in the sand for a while, sobbing, before lifting her head and looking at Jai through the haze of her tears. "If you go, then everyone dies."

Glenda glared at Jai then turned back to Patsy and said, "You don't look capable of stopping anything to me. And you still haven't answered my question. Who are you really?"

Jai ignored his mother and asked, "How do you know what I'm planning to do?"

"Because we already did it. You came back to my time." Patsy reflected on all that had happened, sifting through the events, searching for the right ones to mention, the ones most likely to be believed. "We found your sister, and the Book of Wisdom. The Nasqa were keeping her hidden at the Art Gallery, fifteen years from now. We went in there to try and get her back."

"And?" asked Glenda.

"The consequences…"

"Urgh… you'll have to do better than that."

"I can prove it." Patsy held up the phone.

Glenda held her hand up behind her shoulder, ready to strike. "I'm running out of patience."

Patsy struggled to her feet, holding the phone as high as she could. "When Jai came through the portal, he used this as proof of who he was." She extended her arm toward Glenda, offering her the phone.

"Drop it now, or so help me… I'll blast you right back into that pool you came out of."

"Give it a rest, Mum." Jai stepped forward and reached out to take the phone.

"You gave it to me just before I left, so we could stay in touch."

Jai took the phone and unlocked it. He looked at the log of call records. Then he checked the photos. "I think you'd better look at this, Mum."

CHAPTER 8

Patsy blinked and found herself at the top of the stairs leading down to the pool. She heard a little giggle followed by Clara's voice. "It wouldn't be a surprise if I tell you."

Patsy looked over her shoulder to see Clara carrying a picnic basket. "Is it a book? A book about biology?"

Clara stopped in her tracks. "I must say, you never cease to amaze me." She pulled the book out from the basket and handed it to Patsy. "It's by a scientist called Charles Darwin. It's called *On the Origin of Species.*"

Patsy smiled as she took the book.

She was back.

By preventing Jai from making his journey, she'd been snapped back to the moment before he arrived. She was in a dress, and she felt clean. Yet the memories of what had happened raced around her head.

"Are you okay?" asked Clara.

"Yes, I'm fine, thank you. I'm just so overwhelmed that somehow you must have guessed I've been secretly longing to learn more about biology."

Clara smiled. "I can't begin to tell you what a relief it is to hear you say that. I know how much you love physics, but I really wanted to help you expand your horizons."

Patsy threw her arms around Clara. "Thank you. You're the best tutor a girl could ever hope for."

*

Patsy watched from behind a bush at the bottom of the paddock as Gladys Taylor's sulky arrived. Her father, mother, and tutor waited on the front veranda steps to greet her.

There was something that wasn't right. She shouldn't have accepted her parents' suggestion that she make herself scarce during the woman's visit. She had to go back up there, in case something went wrong. She liked Miss Jenkins too much to see her forced to endure an inquisition from that crabby old monster without Patsy's support. She stood up to make her way up to the house. She was about to take her first step when she heard a voice from behind her. "We need to talk."

She turned and responded to the wood-elf. "Okay, but first, I need to make sure nothing goes wrong for my family."

"They'll be fine. We need to talk, now!" In that instant, they were both transported to Krinkle-myst's cabin

"I did what you asked. I went back and stopped Jai."

"Yes, you did. And, I must say, you did it well. You demonstrated that you do actually listen, after all." He took a seat by the fire and gestured for Patsy to do the same.

"So, why is it so urgent that we talk now?"

"A change you triggered in another timeline will now have to be followed through. You've repaired the damage done before, to this world, and countless others. But that repair is fragile, to say the least."

"But why is it so urgent to tell me this now?"

"Because the events playing out now at your home must take place. In order for this timeline to line up with another. Otherwise, the fabric of reality will start to unravel again, but starting from a different time and place where it would be impossible to repair the damage." He took a sip from a goblet of warm mead that appeared in his hand while he talked. "You need to understand that reality, all of it, is an illusion. That's why it's so fragile, and why it's so malleable to those who understand the science behind it."

"Why are you telling me this now?"

"Because the prophecies of another world have said that the Enchantress shall return. The history of that future is already in place. If it is not fulfilled, reality, as you understand it, will cease to exist. And there are dark forces that work tirelessly to make that come to pass. The Enchantress must return."

Patsy's shoulders slumped. The burden of being a Crossworld Witch weighed heavily on her. *I haven't even taken the same oath as Mother or Nana-Neri. It's not fair.*

"Of course it's fair!"

"Don't you think it's rude to read people's minds?"

"Not when they scream their thoughts out so loud."

"All I want right now is to spend time with Miss Jenkins and my family. I want to be like a normal girl for a while."

"A normal girl, huh? A totally normal girl with an insatiable appetite for knowledge about physics and biology rather than needlework and flower arranging?"

"I've seen the future. It will be normal, and only having an interest in needlework would be awful. I can't imagine what could be worse."

Krinkle-myst nodded and smiled. He liked the young woman Patsy was growing into. "Don't worry, you'll have plenty of time to spend with your family and tutor before the Enchantress must return. In the meantime, the best way to prepare yourself will be to enjoy life."

"So, when the time comes, how will I find my way back there?"

"The way back will find you."

Patsy looked around. The cabin and the wood-elf were gone. She was back at the bottom of the paddock. She looked up to the house just in time to see Gladys Taylor's sulky disappearing from view.

.

Colin grabbed his flintlock and walked out to the veranda when he heard the sound of the approaching horses. His heart sank at the sight of Captain Taylor and six other soldiers, no doubt all controlled by Nasqa. "Captain Taylor, I can't say that it's a pleasure to see you."

"Nor I, you murdering bastard."

"I beg your pardon."

Captain Taylor glanced across at the rider next to him. "Arrest this man and clap him in irons." He turned back to Colin. "This time I promise, you will hang."

Neridah and Meredith raced onto the veranda as one soldier took Colin's flintlock and the other attached irons to his wrists and ankles. Meredith glared at Captain Taylor. "What's happening?"

Captain Taylor ordered his soldiers, "You can arrest these two as well, as accessories."

Patsy appeared at the door, accompanied by Clara. "Let them go!"

"Corporal, if that girl so much as raises a finger, I want you to shoot her father." The corporal raised a pistol, held it up next to Colin's temple, and pulled back the safety.

Patsy glared at the Captain, watching his shadow as it seemingly mocked her. She cast her gaze across all the gathered soldiers. "Nasqa, all of you."

Meredith looked at Clara's puzzled expression, then turned to Patsy. "Patricia! Discretion, remember?"

Clara looked between the two, unable to comprehend what Meredith was talking about.

Neridah whispered to Meredith, "I think the time for secrets has passed. It's time to act."

Meredith nodded and reached out to take hold of Colin's hand. "We'll ride to Sydney and appeal to the Governor."

Captain Taylor laughed. "Please, by all means. I'm sure that would make the Governor's day." He turned to his troops, encouraging them to join him in laughing off the suggestion. The corporal joined in the laughter, lowering his pistol for a moment.

They had to take advantage of this opportunity, or they may not get another. Neridah reached back to take Patsy's hand and gave her a knowing nod while reaching out to take Meredith's at the same time. Patsy raised her free hand and took hold of Clara's.

One of the soldiers asked, "What are they doing?"

Captain Taylor's eyes filled with rage when he realised what was happening.

"Now!" said Neridah.

The corporal raised his pistol's muzzle back to Colin's head and pulled the trigger.

The bullet ricocheted off the hardwood post of the veranda. Colin, the witches, and Clara had vanished.

.

Clara collapsed into a high back leather chair in the library. "What just happened?"

Neridah replied, "We'll explain later." She turned to Patsy. "Drawing the Nasqa out of them, how do you do it?"

Patsy shrugged her shoulders. "It's like allowing yourself to be somewhere, you just let it happen. It's only hard if you try. It's throwing them into the void that's harder."

"We won't have time for that part. We'll need to hope the soldiers are strong enough to block them getting back in." Neridah looked at Meredith. "It's our only chance. We need to split up and keep moving so they're confused. We can pick them off, one by one."

They could hear boots on the floorboards just inside the front door. A soldier's voice called out. "Show yourselves, I know you're in here somewhere."

Colin grabbed a pistol from the drawer of his desk. He looked at his wife and daughter. Sending them into harm's way went against every ideal he held dear, but he knew there was no other choice. "Go, I'll see to it that Miss Jenkins is kept safe."

Clara gasped and held a hand to her breast when the witches vanished. "Surely, this is some mad dream."

Colin stood in front of her, his arm raised, pointing the pistol at the closed library door. "I wish, for all our sakes, that could be the case."

*

The Nasqa inhabiting Captain Taylor could sense Patsy's jump as she moved from the library to be standing in the front doorway. He pulled out his pistol as he turned to face her, but she was already gone. Her presence was close, he could feel it. Then came the tap at his shoulder. As he turned to face her, Patsy reached into his chest and pulled out the Nasqa. Holding the shadowy phantom aloft, she said, "I could so easily open the void and send you there, but I'll show you mercy if you promise to leave this world and never return."

You speak of mercy? Patricia McIntyre dares to speak of mercy? You don't know the meaning of the word.

Resisting the temptation to open the void, Patsy flung the Nasqa aside. "I don't have time for this." She looked down at the Captain, who'd collapsed to the floor "Don't let it back in. It can't take you over again if you actively refuse. I need you to stand guard at the door and make sure none of the others enter the house. Do you understand?"

Captain Taylor was still looking to the floor as he nodded in agreement. By the time he looked up, Patsy was gone.

*

The Nasqa slipped through the door to the library as it sought a new host. There was no point trying Colin, as delicious as that irony would be. His steadfast determination in this moment made his mind an impenetrable fortress. But the young woman? She was anxious and filled with uncertainty and fear. Her mind was like an open door.

Clara was mopping tears from her eyes with an embroidered handkerchief as she struggled to take in breaths between her sobs. *How can this be happening? What the hell is going on? How can any of this be real?*

A voice in the back of her mind reached out with soothing words. *Relax a little, and all will be clear.* From Clara's perspective, it was a welcome suggestion.

*

Jimmy and Darcy O'Sullivan were tending the horses in the stables when the thundering of hoofs heralded the arrival of Captain Taylor and his troops. Jimmy put a hand to his chest, feeling the scar he still bore from the last time Captain Taylor's troops had visited the McIntyre property. They walked out into the paddock and watched as the discussion between Colin and the Captain unfolded with the witches and Clara in the background. Darcy asked, "Should we go up there and see if they need a hand?"

Before Jimmy had a chance to answer, the McIntyre ensemble had vanished. The Captain raced inside while the other soldiers scattered. "By all the saints in heaven, what just happened?"

"They ran inside. Didn't you see?"

Jimmy shook his head. "No one moves that fast." He started walking toward the house but was distracted by the sound of a sulky entering the property. A soldier was driving it and Vincent Donaldson was onboard, battered and in chains. Jimmy turned to Darcy. Father and son exchanged a knowing look then started running to Vincent's aid. The soldier turned the sulky and charged at Jimmy while reaching back to grab a rifle. Darcy, adrenalin pumping, moved quickly. He grabbed the soldier around the shoulders and dragged him from the driver's seat, taking his rifle as the soldier fell to the ground. Jimmy managed to clamber on board and brought the sulky to a stop, then looked up to see an approaching soldier raise his rifle.

"Put your hands up behind your head and dismount, now."

Neridah appeared behind the soldier and tapped him on the shoulder. He turned. Horror filled his eyes as Neridah reached into his chest and pulled out the shadowy Nasqa. It thrashed about in her hands, desperate to break free. Four of the remaining soldiers were running toward the sulky. The fifth had collapsed after Meredith had torn out his tormentor.

Neridah lifted the soldier's chin. "Be strong, don't give it a chance to find its way back in."

Jimmy watched on as Patsy appeared in front of the charging soldiers, causing them to hesitate. She reached into one soldier's chest with her left hand and into another's with her right. At the same time, the other two found themselves face to face with Neridah and Meredith.

A woman's voice called out from the top of the hill. "Stop!" The three witches looked up and saw Clara and Colin standing on the veranda. Clara holding Colin's revolver to his head. "If any one of you so much as moves, or vanishes, so help me, I will shoot."

Patsy stared at Clara, fully aware it was the Nasqa she'd just before shown mercy to who was talking through her tutor. She looked at the revolver and focused, visualising it in the emptiness of the void. She closed her eyes. The image was clear. She reopened them and smiled. Clara was shocked when the weight of the weapon was gone from her hand. Colin turned to her and said, "I suggest you leave Miss Jenkins in peace." He looked at his daughter, who was walking up to the house wearing a heavy frown, then turned back to Clara. "I really don't think you want to be facing my daughter again."

Clara said, "This isn't over, I will be back." With that, the Nasqa drifted from Clara's body and disappeared into a neighbouring crossworld.

Clara fainted and fell, Colin catching her before she hit the deck of the veranda.

Jimmy watched in horror as it all unfolded, triggering memories of what had occurred the year before. Memories that he'd so far managed to suppress. He resolved in that moment that it was time for he and Darcy to look for work in Sydney.

CHAPTER 9

Destellie knocked at the door of the McIntyre homestead. She was looking out at the rising full moon when Meredith answered the door. "Hello, Destellie. Are you nervous about tomorrow?"

Destellie looked coy as she gave a little giggle. "I guess so. I can't quite believe that this time tomorrow I'll be a married woman."

Meredith took Destellie's hands in hers. "We're all so happy for you."

"Thank you. And thank you for agreeing to join me tonight. I can't imagine a better way to enjoy my final night as a single woman than dancing around a fire with my wonderful bridesmaids."

Patsy came running down the stairs calling out, "Come on, Nana-Neri. Desttie's already here." Patsy ran out the front door and threw her arms around Destellie. The bride-to-be swept her up and swung her around.

"How blessed am I to have such a wondrous greeting?"

Colin and the Reverend came out of the library as Neridah descended the stairs, pulling on her gloves. The Reverend looked at Neridah in her emerald-green velvet dress with black lace trim. "That's a good deal of trouble you've gone to for a dance by the fire."

Neridah grinned as she flicked a glove his way. "Oh, do be quiet. A dance by the fire's as good a reason as any to dress up."

As the three of them reached the door, Colin said, "Jimmy tells me that Darcy will be playing his harmonica for you."

Meredith said, "It's so sad that they'll be leaving after the wedding."

Colin nodded. "Yes, but can you blame him? He's doing what he believes is best for Darcy. That's what's guided his decisions for as long as I've known the man."

Cook's voice called from the end of the corridor. "Thank goodness I caught you before you'd left." She hurried along the corridor carrying a wicker basket with a tea towel draped over the top. "When I learned of your plans, I took it upon myself to prepare a pot of soup for you." She handed the basket to Destellie. "There's also bread and cheese in there." She looked Destellie up and down. "Can I get you a blanket? You'll likely catch a chill wearing that skimpy dress and shawl."

Destellie took the basket and gave Cook a warm smile. "Thank you so much, Cook. I'll be fine. Darcy told me he'd be spending the day collecting wood for the fire and I rarely feel the cold, but I do appreciate your concern." She turned to Patsy, Meredith and Neridah. "Shall we go?"

Meredith turned to Colin. "Can I trust you and Alfred to be sensible while we're gone?"

"We'll be fine, we have much to discuss."

The Reverend slapped a hand on Colin's shoulder. "Aye, like whether it's brandy or rum that better warms the soul while playing a meaningful game of checkers."

Patsy turned and looked toward the entrance to the property when she heard the sound of a horse pulling a sulky. "It's Mr Donaldson."

Meredith glanced at Cook. "I think it's time you take that apron off and enjoy your night off."

Cook blushed as she hurriedly removed the apron. "Is there anything else you'll be needing before I go?"

Colin reached across and grabbed the apron out of her hands. "Cook, you need to go now, and make sure you have a good time. I'll be most disappointed if we see you back here before Monday morning."

"Thank you, Mr McIntyre, sir. I'll do my best to enjoy myself, sir."

As Cook made her way down to meet Vincent, Neridah lit a hurricane lamp that sat on a small table by the front door. She held it up and asked, "Shall we make our way down, ladies?"

The moon had risen above the treeline as the witches and Destellie made their way down the paddock. The Reverend's eyes followed with Neridah as she held up the lamp to light the way. Colin said, "It's not too late, you know. No one will hold it against you if you recant your vows."

The Reverend's eyes remained locked on the only woman he'd ever loved. "It wouldn't be fair to her. Physically, I'm forty years her senior."

"Maybe you should let her be the judge of how fair it would be." Colin turned and made his way back into the house, unaware the man he'd just spoken to was in fact his father-in-law. The Reverend stared into the darkness, wondering about what might have been if events had played out differently in his youth.

.

Felibrey was glad for the full moon. It would be enough light for him to nail the last of the roof shingles in place so the cottage would be weatherproof in time for the first night he and Destellie would spend together as husband and wife. It took him by surprise when he climbed the ladder and found Mrs Smith waiting for him on the roof. "You don't deserve this."

Felibrey blushed. "I know, she's so amazing. I still struggle to believe that such a woman would want to commit to a life shared with one such as myself."

The old fairy smacked a hand against her forehead. "Urgh! That's not what I meant. You deserve better." She leaned forward to make a point of staring into his eyes. "You poor, lovesick fool. You've been around for how many thousands of years, and you still don't see what's going on?"

"I don't understand."

"You've been played for a fool. The frogs and crickets have been gossiping about it for weeks."

"What do mean?"

"I mean, your fiancé has been meeting with Kerridwen in secret. This marriage is just a ruse… a means of luring the witches into a trap, which is playing out right now."

"That can't be, the hunter is long gone."

"Oh no. I can assure you, she is fighting to find a way back. She promised Destellie a garland of power in exchange for leading the witches to her… tonight, while the moon is full."

Felibrey opened his mouth to respond, but no words came. He clung tight to the ladder as his world crumbled to dust around him.

*

Darcy sat on a rock by the fire playing an Irish ballad on his harmonica while watching Destellie and the witches descend the stairs. The flames danced as though in time to his music, a plethora of frogs providing a steady rhythm.

Destellie opened her arms and spun around on reaching the bottom of the stairs. "What a beautiful night to dance in the moonlight."

Meredith pulled her shawl tight around her and approached the fire. "It's a bit chilly for me to dance. I think I'll settle for warming myself by the fire."

Patsy skipped across the sand. "I'll dance with you, Desttie. I so love to dance. Come on, Nana-Neri."

Neridah slipped her shoes off at the bottom of the stairs. "I must admit the feeling of the sand underfoot is quite nice."

Destellie danced in a sweeping arc, then reached out and took Neridah's hand. "Yes, it's so soothing." She pulled Neridah along as Darcy stepped up the tempo. "It's wonderful to feel so alive."

Patsy looked across the fire at her grandmother and giggled, then did a pirouette as she passed Meredith. "Come on, Mother, dance with us."

Darcy rose up to his feet and beckoned Meredith to join them as he took his place in the procession dancing around the flames. Their pace quickened, and Meredith began to feel intoxicated as they all twirled around her again and again. She wasn't aware of when she'd thrown her shawl aside, but she was now dancing with them.

None of them had noticed the vortex beginning to form in the centre of the pool.

•

Felibrey ran to the stables, straight to the stall of a black stallion that had only recently been broken in. He grabbed the lead rope as he entered the stall, then jumped on the horse's back, threaded the rope through the halter, and kicked his heels into the massive stallion's side, driving it into the night.

He leaned forward as the horse thundered down the road away from the small village that had grown around the church as the Reverend's disciples had built their homes. "We must fly like the wind, my dear friend."

After what felt like little more than a minute to Felibrey, they reached the bridge that crossed the creek upstream from the McIntyre property. Felibrey pulled hard on the left of the reins. The stallion responded by leaping off the bridge, hooves causing wild splashes as it began navigating its way down the creek.

Water and mud flew up into Felibrey's face and he had to duck so his head was against the horse's neck on many occasions to avoid low lying branches. In the thousands of years he'd been alive, he'd never before been consumed by such a sense of urgency. It didn't matter that Destellie had betrayed him. She was in danger. He had to reach her before she was lost to him forever.

·

Jimmy O'Sullivan walked across to the stables. He was anxious to ensure he had everything packed and ready so he and Darcy could make their way to Sydney after the celebrations had finished. He smiled at the distant sound of laughter from the pool at the bottom of the paddock. It was good that Darcy was enjoying himself on what would be their last night at the property. Then something struck him. The tunes Darcy were playing bore no resemblance to anything Jimmy had heard him play before.

Curious, he made his way down the paddock to take a closer look. On reaching the bottom he peered through the trees, trying to make out what was happening. He felt a tightness in his chest, reminding him of the gunshot wound he'd received a year earlier when Kerridwen had tried to take his son away from him. Blood pulsed in his temples. He raced down the pathway as quick as his legs would carry him.

*

Patsy had never enjoyed dancing so much. They were all holding hands now. She looked at Darcy and marvelled at how he could play the harmonica so well with no hands holding the instrument. How was that even possible? The chorus of the frogs, the screeching of the flying foxes, and the crackling of the fire filled the background as well as any orchestra could. The tempo built and they all threw themselves further into the dance. Meredith was laughing with delight. Neridah's eyes were closed as she lost herself in the celebration. The flames rose higher and spiralled their way into the night sky. The vortex in the pool threw up a waterspout that wound its way into the centre of the dancers, weaving between the flames in a perfect harmony of fire and water. The very air itself joined the circling dancers, creating a wind that moved with them, lifting them off the ground. Each of them rose up and down in a random pattern that mimicked the flickering of the flames. Their laughter grew louder as the pace increased.

The water and flames crept together, weaving through each other to form a shape... the shape of a woman... the shape of Kerridwen, the hunter.

The image of the hunter laughed.

A sound like thunder in the distance merged with the music of the night like a drum roll anticipating a musical crescendo. Kerridwen's sculptured image of pulsating fire and water called to the dancers,

"Come to me now. Come to me and become one with my garland of power."

The dancers picked up speed, moving so fast they became a blur as they drifted in toward the centre. The hunter's image laughed louder as she spread her arms, ready to embrace the dancers and pull them into her garland.

The thundering drum roll grew louder. Then it became clear. Kerridwen realised too late. The drum roll wasn't thunder but the sound of an approaching stallion. She turned to face it as Felibrey compelled the majestic horse to leap into the midst of the spiralling flames and water. The collision triggered a flash of lightning and a deafening crack of genuine thunder. The image of Kerridwen was split down the middle, as is a tree when struck by lightning. Felibrey leapt from his mount and grabbed hold of Destellie, pulling her to ground. The image of Kerridwen pulled itself back together, rage writ large upon her face.

Darcy and the witches continued their dance. But their momentum had slowed so they appeared more to be spinning about in a dazed frenzy.

Jimmy O'Sullivan burst onto the beach, reached up and grabbed hold of his son's leg and pulled him down to the ground. With the circle broken, the witches fell, only to be swept up again as the flames and water reshaped themselves. The ground shook. The flames flickered in and out of the semblance of Kerridwen with the witches spinning around like leaves caught in the wind. The stallion reared up, fearful of what was taking place. Felibrey leapt up and grabbed hold of the reins then managed to clamber onto the great beast's back. "Come, my friend. One more time and we'll be rid of her." He willed the horse to leap into the flames once more.

Kerridwen screamed, "Damn you all!"

An explosion erupted as she blew apart, sending all of them flying back. Jimmy was flung hard against a nearby tree. The water receded, flickering ashes rose up, drifting in and out of a vague semblance of the hunter. Kerridwen's voice was unmistakable in the crackling remnants of the fire. "I will see to it that you suffer as you serve me, you pathetic little witches."

Neridah rose to her feet and reached back to draw energy from the Crossworlds. Patsy grabbed her hand and said, "No, that's what she wants. It's like last time. She's weak. She's trying to goad us into using our powers against her so she can absorb them." Patsy approached the remains of the fire.

Kerridwen laughed, "You think you can be rid of me that easily, witch? Or should I say, Enchantress?" Patsy kicked sand into the flames. Kerridwen laughed again. "You'll serve me yet, little Patsy." The laughter continued, becoming less and less until its last vestiges were extinguished along with the last of the embers.

Colin's voice boomed from the top of the path. "What's happened here?" Patsy looked up to see her father and the Reverend coming down the steps holding a lantern. Neridah ran up to the Reverend, who took her in his arms and held her tight. Colin saw his wife sitting by Darcy while Jimmy lay unmoving on the ground. He raced to be by her side. Darcy was wailing, tears streaming down his cheeks.

"I'm sorry, Dad. I'm so sorry…"

Meredith held Jimmy's wrist. She looked at Darcy and realised there were no words she could offer that would provide any comfort.

Colin asked, "Is there anything you can do for him?"

Meredith shook her head. She grabbed Colin's arm. "There's no pulse, and he's stopped breathing." She buried her face in Colin's shoulder and wept.

Destellie's cry echoed through the night. "Help me, please, somebody!"

They all turned and saw that she was trying to pull Felibrey's limp body from underneath that of the stallion in the shallows of the pool. The Reverend and Colin went to her aid and worked together in silence to pull his lifeless body free.

Destellie was inconsolable. "I'm so sorry. This is all my fault. My beautiful Felibrey... what have I... how did this..."

The Reverend put a hand on her shoulder. "Blaming yourself won't bring him back, and it won't do anything to help you. There were many forces at play here." He looked across at Darcy, whose eyes betrayed his sense of guilt. He turned back to Felibrey's fiancé. "You and the boy were merely pawns. No one here will hold either of you responsible, that is a promise."

.

Patsy ran up the stairs, Meredith calling after her, "Patricia, where do you think you're going?"

She stopped and yelled at her mother, "He should have warned me!"

"Who?"

Tears ran down Patsy's face as she cried out, "You wouldn't understand." She turned from her mother and continued up the stairs.

"Patricia, come back!" Meredith started walking toward the stairs but then felt Colin's firm grip on her shoulder.

"Let her go." Colin whispered in his wife's ear. "She's been through so much. She needs to let it out. Don't worry, she'll be back."

Meredith took Colin's hand and held it against her cheek as she nodded in agreement.

*

Patsy raced along the bottom of the paddock. "Krinkle-myst! Let me in! Let me in! I need to talk to you!"

She reached the spot where the portal would normally appear, only to find there was the same darkness there as the surrounding bush. "Krinkle-myst!" Patsy looked up at the night sky and screamed at the moon and stars, "Where are you!" She fell to her knees. "Why didn't you warn me?" Her vision was blurred by the flood of tears, her voice choking on her sobs. "I could have saved them." She buried her face in her hands and kept repeating, "I could have saved them…"

"You don't know that."

Patsy looked up. She was in Krinkle-myst's cabin, next to his fireplace. The wood-elf was sitting at his writing desk with his back to her. "Why?" she asked.

"Why what?" The movement of his quill suggested he was more concerned about his writing than about Patsy's questions.

"Why didn't you warn me? I could have saved them. They didn't need to die."

"You don't know that."

"You could have warned me. Now Felibrey and Jimmy are dead… why?"

Krinkle-myst's quill stopped moving. "What was it you said to your mother just a moment ago? Oh, that's right… you wouldn't understand." The quill started its movement across the page again.

Patsy blinked and found she was back in the paddock with nothing but the sound of crickets around her. She got to her feet, her mind feeling empty as she traipsed back to the pathway. It was as though there was no room left for any kind of thoughts or feelings in her head. She'd never felt quite so numb.

The young witch worked her way down the stairs, wanting to wake up from this nightmare. She looked down at Destellie wailing over Felibrey's body and Darcy clinging to his dead father. A grim realisation flooded through her. She finally understood why her mother had hidden the truth from her about their family when she was younger. She understood why she'd wanted to protect her from the burden they carried, and why she'd hoped Patsy would never need to learn of it.

Meredith met her daughter at the bottom of the stairs. Patsy buried herself in the warmth of her mother's embrace.

EPILOGUE

Patsy turned to Clara as they walked down the path to the pool, the tutor carrying a picnic hamper. "I got a letter from Darcy yesterday."

"Oh, how is he?" asked Clara.

"He started a new job last week. He's learning to be a carpenter."

"That's nice. Do you think he's happy?"

"I hope so. Mother and Nana-Neri said he can never be happy here after what happened last year."

Clara paused and took a deep breath. She tried to avoid thinking about those events—events that had challenged everything she'd ever understood about the world. She gave a gentle nod and said, "I think they're quite right in that regard."

"Oh, and he said he ran into Bordauex. Apparently, the archbishop has taken a great interest in the Reverend Casey's work and wants to travel up here soon to meet with him."

"Oh? Well that should be interesting."

Ferdinand came running down the steps, catching up to them as they reached the bottom of the pathway. Patsy picked him up then asked, "Miss Jenkins, would it be okay if I call you Clara? I feel like you're more of a friend than a tutor now."

Clara smiled and said, "I'd like that very much, but not in front of your parents."

They made their way to the rock where they always sat for their picnics. Patsy noticed the corner of a dark, rectangular metal object sticking out of the sand near the edge of the pool. She raced down and picked it up, brushing the sand off it. Jai's phone!

"What is it?" asked Clara.

"Oh, just something I thought I'd lost."

"Show me."

Patsy looked over her shoulder. She blushed as she kept the phone hidden from view. "I'd rather not, if that's okay. To be honest, it's a little embarrassing."

"Ah!" Clara gave a knowing smile. "I kept diaries like that when I was your age. Don't worry, I won't pry."

Shielding the phone from Clara's view, Patsy turned it on, remembering all the step-by-step instructions Jai had given her like it was yesterday. Her intuition told her to tap the text message icon.

There was a photo of Jai with his mother and little sister standing next to the Book of Wisdom, on its stand in the library where it belonged.

Patsy smiled at the image then scrolled down to read Jai's message.

> *Hi Patricia,*
>
> *I just wanted to thank you. Mum and I followed up on your tip about the gallery, and you were right. It took a year of planning, but we got Mel back last week, and the Book of Wisdom. Ever since you talked me out of our original plan, I've been having the craziest dream about what would have happened if you hadn't stopped me. The bit that always stands out the most is where we end up meeting the legendary Krinkle-myst and he lectures us about future history. I'd love to know if maybe you've had the same dream.*

Patsy closed her eyes and bit down on her lower lip while holding the phone to her chest. When she opened her eyes, she smiled and hurled the phone into the middle of the pool.

Clara called out, "Bravo! Sometimes that's the best way to treat past embarrassments."

Patsy let out a little giggle as she walked back up the beach and sat next to Clara on the rock. "Actually, it's not so much that it's embarrassing, just something I need to put behind me. It's not really something I want to talk about though, if that's okay."

"Of course it is. But as you said, we're friends. So please, if there's ever anything you ever need to talk about, you can trust that it will never go past the two of us."

Patsy threw her arms around Clara. "Thank you."

As Clara started unpacking the picnic basket, she noticed a bit of movement near Patsy's foot. "Is that a leech?"

Patsy looked down and saw how the light refracted as it passed through the waving, over-sized head of the leech-like worm.

The stringworm latched onto Patsy's foot before she had a chance to pull it away.

THE END